The lights were on, second level up front, probably a bedroom. I edged the Toyota to the curb, bent the sideview mirror so I could see the house in it, and slouched down in the seat to wait.

At a quarter to nine the upstairs lights went out. A few seconds later, a light came on downstairs, then one in the garage. The garage door tilted open with a slow-motion hum I could hear even with my window rolled up. In the empty night, I heard a soft purr, then watched as a motorcycle curved out from behind the car and disappeared down the street.

The light went off and the door started to drop with a slow, lumbering pulse. I grabbed my bag, scrambled out of the car, and made it by inches, shoving the bag in first in front of me, then rolling my body flat beneath the garage door just before it swung shut. It had to be the easiest break-in I'd ever done. . . . I'd have to save the Riley for another night, when I could take my time and do it just for the sheer pleasure. . . .

MURDER
ON THE
RUN

Gloria White

A DELL BOOK

Published by
Dell Publishing
a division of
Bantam Doubleday Dell Publishing Group, Inc.
666 Fifth Avenue
New York, New York 10103

ISBN: 0-440-20983-8

Printed in the United States of America

Published simultaneously in Canada

July 1991

10   9   8   7   6   5   4   3   2   1

RAD

For Ramos K.

1

At 6:00 A.M. the path between Crissy Field and the San Francisco Bay was deserted. And it should be, I thought as I ran along the edge of the Bay. It was too early for the walkers to be out, and everybody else who'd run the Bay to Breakers yesterday was at home in bed, nursing runner's knees and hangovers. Lucky them. If I'd finished the race, I'd be asleep, too, instead of working on a runner's high out here, sweating in the cold.

The only sound above the muffled rush of Monday morning bridge traffic and the nearby wash of the waves was the solid *crunch, crunch* of my own frayed running shoes as they hit the gravel underfoot. After a minute I reached the pavement and ran on in silence, letting my mind drift.

For a half-Mexican daughter of jewel thieves, I was doing pretty good with my life: I finally had my P.I. license and, after a year, was actually making a living doing investigations. Knowing the city, being a native San Franciscan, helped, but knowing how to breach security systems—from locks to burglar alarms—helped even more. Since I never take anything except information, I look at it as sort of carrying on the family trade without the guilt. But there was another payoff, too, a reason I knew I'd found my niche: sometimes in a stranger's darkened room, with my lock picks and penlight in hand and my heart beating as fast as a hummingbird's, I'd sense my father's deep-brown Mexican eyes on me and my mom's sparkling Anglo ones, and I'd feel closer to them then than I'd ever felt when they were alive.

With their memory on my mind, I ran past the Coast Guard station and the Park Service outbuildings, then up the canted road that led to Fort Point, the old Civil War relic under the Golden Gate Bridge.

It was there, when I swung out and jogged along the fat yellow line down the center of the road, that I spotted them: two men standing bareheaded against the brisk May wind. They were at the tip of the fort, not more than five feet from where Jimmy Stewart pulled Kim Novak out of the Bay in *Vertigo*. They weren't fishermen or surfers: Neither carried poles or boards, and one man—the big one—had on a suit and tie. The other guy was wearing a blue windbreaker over tan pants.

From the way they were standing, the big man towering over the other one, it looked like the little guy was getting chewed out over something.

I felt uneasy and thought about turning back, but before I could make up my mind, the little guy started shouting. The first couple of words were garbled, but he said something, something else, then "vengeance."

I drew up at the brick portals, about seventy yards away from them, but neither seemed to notice me. They just kept yelling back and forth at each other like I wasn't even there. I looked around for somebody else, but it was just me, them, and the specter of Jimmy Stewart.

Before I knew it, the man in the suit had the little guy by the throat. He jerked him bodily up off the pavement and swung him back and forth, up and down, with vicious little shakes like a terrier would a rat. The little guy flailed his arms and tried to get away, but the big man in the suit paid no attention. He just kept on shaking and swinging. Then suddenly the blue arms went limp. The legs stiffened, then they went limp too.

"Stop! Hey you, stop it!"

The big man looked up at me, surprised. I was surprised myself. Here I was, a woman half his size and about a third his weight, telling him what to do. I didn't know judo or karate or what the hell I was even doing down there. The one thing I did know was that he wasn't happy to see me.

We were close enough to get a good look at each other and that's exactly what the big guy did: he stared at me like he was memorizing my face. I had just enough time to take in his square jaw, dark hair, and streak of white at the temple before he tossed the limp body into the water like an empty candy wrapper and came after me.

He was big as a bear, but a lot of big men could run. *Run.* I wheeled around and sprinted back down the way I'd come. *God, don't let him catch me,* I prayed, and the cold fear inside me made me fly like Pegasus.

I looked over my shoulder once, right before I ducked around the Park Service outbuildings. He was closing the distance, wheezing after me like a locomotive, but I ignored the pain in my side and doubled my speed. I didn't look back again until I dodged behind the high stand of bushes surrounding the Coast Guard station house. I flew up the three steps to the porch and slammed my fist against the door.

"Help! Help! Emergency! Open up!"

My breath came in jagged little gasps as I pounded the polished oak door. I wanted whoever was inside to hear me, but I didn't want the killer to know where I was. *"Hurry, please,"* I whispered.

The latch rattled; the door opened about an inch. I pushed, but the door wouldn't budge. I looked up. A pair of soft blue eyes, narrowed in suspicion, peered out at me.

"What is it?" a woman's voice asked from the other side.

"Please, *please*. You've got to help." I pushed against the door, again. *"Please,* let me in."

She blinked and I knew she was sizing me up, trying to decide if I was going to do something weird to her if she let me in. I guess I looked sane enough because after a second the door swung open. I shoved my way inside. "Quick! Lock it. There's somebody after me."

She released the collar of her pink chenille bathrobe and locked the door while I steadied myself against the wall. I took a couple of deep breaths, then looked her over. She was just under my height, probably five-three, blond, and slender. Not exactly the mounted police, but between the two of us, I figured, we might hold our own. At least until the cops arrived.

The foyer was dark, paneled in knotty pine, and smelled of fresh brewed coffee. It had the cozy, dark feeling of a cabin below deck. I half expected the floor to surge with the lift of a wave, but it didn't. That was okay. It felt warm and safe—temporarily.

"We need to call the police," I said.

She didn't move. "Did someone jump?" The way she said it, clear and slow and patient, sounded like she was talking to a three-year-old.

"Jump?" I stared at her. My mind drew a blank. Then I understood. "No, no, he was pushed. He—"

"Sarah?" a voice called from down the hall. "Sarah, who's down there? Are you all right?"

But Sarah was already bundling a pea jacket over my clammy shoulders and hustling me out the front door.

"Hey, what the—?" I grabbed the doorframe and hung on. Nobody was going to shove me back out there until the cops came.

"The station office is over there," the woman explained, pulling on my arm and pointing to the white clapboard building across the yard. "They'll send out the boats from there," she said. I let go. Over her shoulder she called out to the guy in the house, "Hurry, John. There's a man in the Bay."

We couldn't take the direct route, the one I'd run along, because upright metal bars blocked the entrance, so we drove up a hill, around and back down again. As the Bay came into view, I heard the slow purr of the motorboats. From the way they crisscrossed the water, slowly and systematically like a couple of lawn mowers, I knew they hadn't found what they were looking for.

The jeep skimmed past the brick pillars and took us right up to where the two men had fought.

"Where'd he go in?" the captain asked.

"That's it," I said, and pointed. "Right there. The little guy came from around the building right over there, and the big guy grabbed him by the neck and started choking him, then threw him in. Right here."

We all got out and stood at the end of the paved road, next to the walls of the old fortress, and stared into the frigid water. The guy who sat next to me in the backseat started taking his clothes off and ended up in a yellow wet suit. He put on headgear and a harness, then waited at the edge of the breakwater for somebody to tell him to dive in. Nobody did, though, so he just stood there, shivering in the cold. I thought about what it would be like down there, deep under the water, then pulled my borrowed pea jacket tight and looked at Captain John.

"They haven't found him yet, have they?"

"Not yet." He scanned the choppy bay with clear blue eyes.

"Could he be out there?" I motioned with my chin toward the Pacific, out past the Golden Gate.

"It's possible. We've got a flood tide, but if he goes down deep enough, the crosscurrent could carry him out. It gets as deep as four hundred feet under the bridge, but I doubt he went that far." He stared at the craggy edge of the breakwater where bay met land. "Frankly I'm surprised he's not hung up on these rocks here. If he was unconscious, it would seem likely he would."

I stared past the thick guard chain to the gray waters and tried to think positive thoughts. It didn't work.

"How long before . . . ?"

John checked his wristwatch. "We'll give him another half hour. Nobody can last longer than that out there today. Especially if he went over unconscious."

"Oh."

The noise of the boats churning out there put me on edge, so I turned my back to the water and looked down the road I'd covered twice already that morning. The pavement was damp and shiny from sea spray and, off in the distance near the Park Service buildings, I could make out a couple walking their dog, a collie.

When the dog disappeared up the steep, brush-covered slope that ran parallel to the road, I felt a chill. It had nothing to do with how cold it was. It was like *he* was up there, hiding behind the trees and the bushes, watching me. I turned back to John. "Is anybody looking for the other guy?"

"Sure." On cue a siren sounded in the distance. "They should catch him if he's on his way out."

I kept my eye on the hill, and when the sirens got closer, something up there moved, a quick motion of white at the crest of the slope. I held my breath. He was up there, standing out in the open, bold as a bulldozer. I grabbed John's sleeve.

"Look! Up there. He's up there in the bushes."

"Where?" John swung around, but it was too late. He was gone. "Where?"

"Shit! He's getting away!" I started down the road, but John reached out and stopped me. *"Come on,"* I hissed, fighting his grip. "He's getting away."

"We'll never catch him on foot. They'll do it." He nodded at the police car, now sliding up behind the jeep.

John hurried over to them and pointed up the slope, but before they could pull out to chase the guy down, a second car lurched to a stop behind them. When a third one showed up a few seconds later, I knew we were sunk. John barked a few short words at them, and all three cars took off back up the road. I watched them go—military police, park police, and city police—and knew we didn't have a prayer.

"Don't look so glum," John said. "They can handle it."

"What makes you so sure?"

For the first time that morning, John grinned at me. "You don't have much confidence in bureaucrats, do you?"

"I've got every reason not to," I said. "I used to be one."

2

The bureaucrat that I'd been was a parole officer. I tried it for a couple of years and got to meet a lot of interesting people, most of whom knew, or knew of, my parents. Because I did what I could, ignoring procedures and triplicate forms, I ended up being more popular with the parolees than with the court and prison systems. It all got old very fast, and I finally tired of watching ninety percent of the staff push their papers around and around and around while the rest of us tried to get something done. So I left.

But that was a long three years ago. Now as I looked out across the Bay to the clear view I had of Angel Island and Alcatraz, I tried to forget all the fumbling I'd seen back then. A string of five pelicans glided by, inches above the whitecaps. I watched them until they were pin dots in the sky, then turned back to the chubby cop next to me and hoped against reason that the poor man had a brain.

He was tall and blocky, with the bland features of the not-so-intelligent. His name was Tucker, and he was with

the U.S. Army Military Police. The city cop and the park
police were gone. They'd left an hour ago after flipping a
coin to see who'd write up the report and give copies to
the other two. Tucker lost.

John—I'd found out his last name was Scopes—was
gone too. He had to search for a man in a kayak who'd
disappeared east of Alcatraz.

A few yards from where we stood a pair of surfers
slipped out of their wet suits into long pants and jackets
while Tucker watched, obviously not the least bit bothered by John Scopes's radio message to call off the search.

"Can't you drag the Bay?" I asked.

Tucker blinked. "Do you know how big the Bay is?"

"There must be *something* you can do to find the
body."

"You heard what the Coast Guard said about the cur-
rents. He could be anywhere." He gestured out to sea.
"Out there," he said, then pointed toward Alcatraz, "or
in here. The only sure thing is, you can put your money
on the table he's a goner."

"Is the city going to handle this?"

He frowned and pursed his lips. I guessed he was
thinking.

"It's our jurisdiction," he said after a minute, "but it's
possible we would workshare our expertise in a case like
this."

I nodded. I understood perfectly. He'd never seen anything rougher than a speed bump, so he'd have to turn
the case over to the city's homicide squad.

"Makes sense," I said, but even that wasn't subtle
enough. His smooth face contorted. I think I hurt his
feelings. "I mean, two heads are better than one." *Especially when the first one's IQ is close to zero.*

The surfers threw their gear into a blue van and drove

off. Tucker flipped through the pages of his notebook until he found a blank sheet. He fished a pencil out of his breast pocket, licked the tip with his tongue, and said, "I gotta ask some questions. Name?"

"Ronnie—Veronica—Ventana. I'm thirty-three, single, divorced and I live over on Grant Avenue." I gave him the address and my phone number. "That's home *and* work," I said.

He scribbled furiously, asked me to repeat the phone number twice, the address three times, then looked up and frowned. "You done this before?"

I nodded. "I'm a private investigator and I do—"

"Whoa! Hold on."

I waited for him to jot that down before I said anything else. "I do burglar-alarm consulting. I'm—"

"Dammit! Hold on. Burglar . . . alarm . . . consulting." He said each word out loud while he wrote it. Then he looked up. "Okay."

"I'm not on a case now and I like to run every chance I get. This morning looked good, so I came out. Then I saw the two men arguing, saw the one throw the other in the water and come after me, so I ran. The Coast Guard called it in for me, and here we are."

"Let's go over that again." He wrote for another five minutes, stopping after every other word to read me what he'd written so far and ask, "And then what?" Finally he finished and asked me for descriptions.

"The little guy—the victim—looked about my height, maybe taller, so say around five-five. And he was skinny, maybe one-twenty, one-thirty, straight dark hair, sort of shaggy, no facial hair. Tan pants, blue windbreaker." I gave it to him two words at a time, waiting each time until he looked up for more before going on.

"The other man was huge. Six-two, maybe six-four, I

can't be sure. At least two hundred pounds, wavy black hair, white streak in it at the left temple. No facial hair either. Black suit, tie, white shirt."

"What else?"

I shrugged. "I can't think of anything else. What about you?"

"Nah. Too bad we didn't nail him." Tucker sounded like he thought the possibility was actually within the realm of his capabilities. I knew better than to disillusion him.

"Can I go now?"

Tucker flipped slowly through the pages of his notebook. "You sure about all this?"

"Of course, I'm sure."

"Just don't leave town without letting me know ahead of time."

I rolled my eyes, turned on my heel, and walked slowly down the Golden Gate Promenade toward the Coast Guard station house.

This time I used the shiny brass knocker on the polished oak door and noticed the Stop Burglar Alarm Company sticker in the corner window. Stop Burglar always uses a photoelectric-beam detector with an open-circuit perimeter alarm—a cinch to beat for anybody with a flashlight for the beam and clippers for the wires. The system was practically obsolete, but half the homes in the city had Stop Burglar systems. You'd think somebody'd figure out they didn't work.

A shuffling sound inside let me know someone was coming, so I slipped the borrowed jacket off and waited. The door opened, and I was looking at Sarah Scopes again. She was dressed now: corduroy pants, a sweater, and her pale straight hair tied back in a short ponytail at the base of her neck.

"I brought this back," I said, holding the coat out in front of me.

"Oh. Thanks." She took it from me. "Come on in. You must be freezing."

Inside, the house's warmth washed over my naked legs and arms and felt good. The place still seemed cozy, safe, and vaguely nautical.

Sarah hung the coat up behind the door. "Come on," she said, and started down the hall. I followed her into the kitchen. It was a large, sun-washed room that reminded me of a friendly farmhouse kitchen. The air was pure essence of rich roasted coffee. Sarah pulled a mug out of a cabinet, then pointed to a chair.

"How about some coffee? You must be frozen to the quick." She filled the mug without waiting for an answer and set it down in front of me. "People usually need a cup of something after talking to Tucker." She sat down across from me and wrapped her hands around her own mug. "They didn't find him, did they?"

"No."

"Do you have someone to go home to, someone to talk to?"

"I'll be all right."

"I wish I'd seen something," she said, and I could tell that it really bothered her that she hadn't. She squinted against the sunlight, but her face was smooth and unlined, not weathered like her husband's. Her features had his same honest intelligence. "We were just getting up, and the bushes block nearly everything from the first floor. Even from upstairs we can't see the fort."

"From what your husband said, it probably wouldn't have made any difference."

"Probably not. Did they find the other man? The one who pushed him in?"

I started to answer, but before I could, a rattle behind me made me jump. I turned in time to see a boy of about eight race in through the back door.

"Mommy! Mommy! I saw the baby seal again!" He was wearing blue jeans and a green down jacket, and a pair of red binoculars hung around his neck. The boy was a little blond replica of his mother, all smiles and flushed with excitement, but he skidded to a stop as soon as he saw me.

"I, uh—" He took a step back and looked at me like he'd made a big mistake and wished he hadn't. A dog scratched at the back door and whined, but the kid didn't move; he just stood there like a rabbit frozen under the glare of headlights. I wondered why he was so scared of me, but Sarah didn't seem to notice.

"That's wonderful, darling," Sarah said. "But weren't you supposed to be cleaning up your gear? Where's your sleeping bag? Where's the tent?" Her voice was all good-natured patience. She looked at me. "Johnny likes to camp out in the yard when we don't get a chance to over the weekend. Johnny, this is Miss Ventana."

The kid's eyes were on the leather tips of his Nikes. He hung back, tongue-tied and bashful.

"I like to go camping too," I said. "Ever been up to Big Basin Redwoods?"

He stole a glance at me, then focused back on his shoes and nodded.

"We've tried them all, I think," Sarah said with a laugh. "And John insists on roughing it all the way. No campers, just tents and a backpack."

Out of the corner of my eye I saw the kid slip out the back door while his mother was talking.

"Johnny!"

I'm sure he heard her, but he didn't stop. He just kept on going until he and the dog disappeared up the beach.

"I'm sorry. He—"

"It's all right," I said. "He's probably got things to do." I stood up. "And so do I. Thanks for the coffee."

Sarah shook her head and got up, too, then walked me to the front door. "I hate to sound like a parent," she said, "but he's never this rude. I can't imagine what got into him."

"Thanks, again," I said, and headed up the parking lot toward Crissy Field.

3

I paced myself as I jogged up North Point toward my North Beach apartment. The morning traffic had pretty much cleared, so I ran along the right edge of the pavement, on the street instead of the sidewalk, skirting the long row of parked cars and keeping an ear open for cars coming from behind.

It was weird, but now that I was alone, my mind kept zeroing in not on murder or drowning, but on the hot shower that was waiting for me at home. Somehow I couldn't let go of the thought. I guess I hoped the steamy water would wash the whole morning off my skin and I could stop feeling so bad for the dead man.

I forced myself to think of something else, concentrated on my breathing, and came up with how Tucker had pretty much shot the morning for me. He didn't instill one with much confidence, but maybe somewhere under all that hamburger was a brain.

"Ha!" I said out loud, then missed a step when a sudden rush of hot air pushed me sideways. A blue Volvo, its engine running so smoothly I hadn't heard it come up behind me, missed me by inches. It skidded to a dead stop, blocking my path.

I stumbled, pulled up short, but couldn't stop my legs in time. I smashed into the car's front fender and fell across its hood, breaking the impact with my arms. I pushed myself off quickly, and stared through the windshield at the driver, but all I could see was a man's torso in a business suit—he was already getting out of the car.

I unclenched my teeth. "What the hell—"

"Are you all right?"

I took one look at the driver and went limp. "My God, Mitchell, you almost ran over me!"

The Nordic-blond male hurried around the front of the car while I pulled myself together. He was slender and athletic, about five-eleven, and good-looking except for a too large nose. As usual he was dressed straight from a page out of *Esquire:* my ex.

These days he looked more like the megabucks corporate accountant he was than the rock who helped me get through my parents' death when we were both fifteen. The only remnants of the wild, scruffy kid I'd gone to high school with were the slight bow in his legs and the dancing light in his eyes.

Mitchell always found something to smile about. He never took no for an answer and enjoyed looking after people. We'd been divorced eight years now, five more than we'd been married, and he still occasionally felt like he had a say in my life.

I didn't begrudge him his success—he liked being a "captain of industry"—but he kept trying to get me to buy into the same bag. That's why he was getting harder to take lately. It was also probably why I'd told myself that he kept in touch more than I cared to.

"I was on my way over to see you," he said. "You okay?"

I exhaled. "I'm fine, Mitchell."

"You're sure?" He touched my shoulder solicitously.

"Yes. I'm okay." I smoothed the front of my nylon running shorts and looked up into his earnest face and startling blue eyes. As always, regret washed over me. It wasn't that I wanted to still be married to him; it was just that we'd both tried so hard to make it work: counseling, separations, vacations together, vacations apart. We'd even talked to a priest, but some things just weren't meant to be. Our own synergy had worked like a curse against us.

I still liked a lot of things about Mitch, but they didn't outweigh the bad habits and the bad memories that I didn't care to live with.

"What are you doing out today?" he asked, looking puzzled. "Didn't you do the Bay to Breakers?"

"Sort of. A guy in front of me had a heart attack, so I waited with him for the ambulance. I didn't see much point in finishing after that."

A red station wagon honked as it skirted Mitchell's parked car. "I'd better move this thing," he said. "Let me give you a lift." He opened the passenger door. "You going home?"

"Yes, but—"

"Come on, we can talk."

"Mitch, we're not married anymore. We don't need to talk."

"Sure we do." He winked. "It'll be okay. Come on."

I sighed and got in. The only time Mitch had ever listened to me was when I asked him for a divorce. Everything before and everything since had been just so much wind against a wall. He got in beside me and put the car in gear.

"What do you think?" he asked.

"About what?"

"The car, Ron, the car. I'm testing it out. My mechanic says they're great, but I don't know if I really need another car, do you know what I mean?"

"How many will this make?"

He frowned and shifted uncomfortably. "Five. Listen, what I wanted to see you about was, are you interested in a job?"

"You mean a case?"

He sighed. "A job, Ronnie. A *real* job. Not breaking into people's houses to see if their burglar alarms work and not snooping around looking for someone else's trouble either." He'd never liked any of my careers, not even my job at the parole office. But that one, we both agreed, was all wrong. He thought it was too dangerous and I thought it was too dull. "This job Skipper was telling me about sounds great. It'd be a real chance for you to break out, Ronnie."

"What do you mean?" I knew exactly what he meant. We'd had the same discussion at least once a week when we were married, and once a month since the divorce: I had everything it took to hold down a legitimate nine-to-five job. He never could understand that I didn't *want* a nine-to-five job.

"You know what I mean. Think about the work you've had. The parole office. Locksmith. The burglar alarm company, then hyping people into letting you design security for them 'cause you broke into their house. And now this. Ronnie, none of it strikes me as being real solid."

"And it all boils down to my parents' being irresponsible thieves, right? Look, they didn't show me how to breach my first alarm; I learned all by myself. You know what they taught me? They taught me it's wrong to steal. I know it because *they* told me. Besides, there's a big difference between being a second-story operator and being a P.I." I laughed. "At least the last time I checked there was."

He passed a silver Mercedes and we rode along for a few minutes without saying anything. When he broke the silence, his tone was softer.

"So . . . are you working on a case?"

"I'm doing Myra's Tuxedo Messages while she's on that study thing in Amsterdam."

Mitch smirked. "How'd she rope you into that?"

"She's my cousin, Mitch. What am I supposed to say?"

"What'd she do, forward her phone?"

I nodded.

"No cases, then?"

"I just finished one."

"Yeah?"

As much as Mitch razzed me for being a P.I., he never lacked curiosity about any of my cases. But I didn't want to talk about this last one, at least not right now. Why anybody would go all the way to Genoa, Italy, just to blow his brains out was beyond me. It had been hard enough to talk to the police about it, both there and here, and it had been hell having to tell his daughter, then turn around and charge a fee for tracking him down. I'd collected enough to cover three months' rent, but that was the only good thing I could say about it. It was all still too fresh, too raw.

But I didn't want to hear about any job, either, so instead I did what always worked best with Mitch: I changed the subject. I told him about the murder at Fort Point.

When we pulled up in front of my apartment, a man was emptying cases of Bacardi rum from a double-parked truck in front of the Volvo. My humble two-roomer—if you counted the bathroom—was over the Quarter Moon Saloon. It was modest, but it was mine—all I could afford without taking Mitchell's money.

"Did you get a good look at this guy?" Mitchell asked. He was going into his he-man protective number.

"We had a stare-off for a couple of seconds, yeah."

Mitch set his mouth in a straight line. I knew the look: He had something on his mind but he wasn't sure he should say it. He would. He always did.

"If you got a good view of him, then he must have seen you."

"Look at me, Mitch." I touched the cotton painter's cap on my head. "My hair's stuffed up in this cap, no makeup. I'm all sweaty. He probably thinks I'm a guy."

Mitchell smiled at me. "Not a chance. I recognized you. From the back, no less."

"That's different. You've been looking at me since high school."

"Just do me a favor," he said. "Don't run down there anymore. He could be waiting for you. Do the park or someplace else, okay?"

"Not to worry. This guy is so big I can run laps around him." I laughed and opened the door, but Mitch stopped me with his hand on my arm.

"What are you going to do?"

I'd heard that tone before too. It usually pushed my buttons, but this time the little spark of annoyance died as quickly as it surfaced. Progress. I smiled.

"I'll tell you exactly what I'm going to do. I'm going to

go upstairs, shower, and deliver three Tuxedo messages for Myra. Then I'm going to stuff myself at the American Investigators Association banquet tonight. In other words, Mitch, I'm going to let the police do their job."

4

"So who's the guest speaker tonight?" I asked when I'd finished the last of my "chicken Parmesan." I directed my question to the craggy-featured, gray-haired man on my right.

For a broken-down ex-boxer I'd met in a bar, Blackhand Coogan had turned out to be a pretty good friend. He was seedy and tough and smart and all those neat things private detectives are supposed to be. He, more than anybody else in the crowded banquet hall, looked the part. The rest of the audience was overwhelmingly middle-aged, paunched-out, and male. Roughly a quarter of them had brought dates, but for the most part it was obvious tonight's ritual was considered a strictly male activity. Probably something to do with male bonding.

I set my fork down when Blackie didn't answer. I followed his intense gaze to the cavernous cleavage of an auburn-haired woman at a table across from ours.

"Blackie!" I hissed, then kicked him under the table. "Come out of it. You're going to embarrass yourself."

He blinked, or maybe he was winking at the redhead, I

couldn't tell. Then he rasped out a good-natured chuckle and reached automatically for a cigarette from the ever-present pack inside his breast pocket.

"Fuck," he said, drawing a flame from his lighter. "Nothing embarrasses me, doll. You ought to know that by now." He turned clear blue take-me-as-I-am eyes on me and smiled confidently. "I think she was enjoying it as much as me."

As if to confirm what he'd just said, the redhead raked me with her eyes, then melted the daggers into a come-on look that nearly drew Blackie out of his chair.

He was the only sixty-five-year-old I'd ever met who had so much sex appeal you could smell it from across the room. Women came on to him as though he were a millionaire. But even though the attraction was there between the two of us, he never came on to me. "Business and pleasure," he'd said when I asked him about it one time, "are water and oil. Don't try to mix them 'cause they won't."

He stretched his arm around the back of my chair and smiled. "What's on your mind, doll?"

"Who's going to talk tonight?" I tried hard to ignore the redhead, but he was making it tough. "Blackie! Stop staring at her. She's going to be in your lap in a minute."

He laughed, blowing smoke out over our heads. "Don't worry. She looks too much like Shirley. I'll never make that mistake twice." He stubbed out his cigarette, swallowed the last of his beer, and said, "Pete August."

"What?"

"That's who's talking tonight."

"Is he the guy who used to work for the D.A.'s office?"

"Yeah. And the P.D. too. And now he's a P.I." Blackie stifled a belch. "I don't like him. He's too slick."

I leaned back so the waiter could clear my plate. "There's nothing wrong with that," I said.

"Nah, I guess not." He threw his napkin down and pushed his chair back. "You done? Let's get out of here."

Blackie wasn't much at socializing. He came mostly for the meals. His idea of a good time was being holed up in somebody's basement drinking beer and listening to a jazz jam until two in the morning. I didn't like hanging around much, either, especially with these potbellied old farts, but I'd heard a lot of good things about August. He had a sharp mind, a cunning instinct, and a track record that included solving two of the city's highest profile crimes—the murder of a police commissioner ten years ago and the kidnapping of a billionaire's son last year. August was supposed to be slick, as Blackie put it, but that was okay as long as he shared some technique with us. Besides, he was the most relevant speaker they'd had all year.

I pulled Blackie back down into his chair. "Hold on. Let's see what he's got to say."

Blackie scowled and got up again. "For what? Just 'cause he's connected doesn't mean he knows more'n me."

"Can't teach an old dog new tricks, is that it?"

Blackie scowled again and sat back down. "You want to stay, we'll stay. But the guy's nobody. The only way he got ahead was by playing his connections."

I settled in my chair as the announcer approached the podium and tapped the microphone. His introduction seemed to go on forever, but the audience didn't mind. They weren't listening anyway. Most sat with their backs to the podium and raised their voices to be heard over the microphone. Too much free beer. Poor August. He wouldn't stand a chance. And neither would I. I pushed my chair back and picked up my purse.

"I guess you're right. We won't be able to hear anything anyway. Let's go."

Blackie grinned. "Smart move. I'm with you, babe." Taking my elbow, he guided me through the maze of tables.

We were halfway to the door when an odd, gnomish man rose from a table in front of us. He held a small plastic mask over his mouth and waved with his other hand.

"Blackie! Blackhand Coogan!" he gasped, then covered his face with the mask again. It was attached by a long tube to a small green canister at his feet. He looked like one of the winos from Market Street: unkempt, bleary-eyed and unshaven, but Blackie had introduced me to even stranger-looking people. I stopped.

"Look, Blackie. That man knows you."

"Where?"

I pointed, and when Blackie spotted him, his face hardened. "Shit. What's that little snitch doing here?"

He pivoted and kept on walking. The "little snitch" caught up with us anyway, lugging his miniature air tank with him.

"Blackie, old boy!"

Blackie stopped and sneered down at the little man, but didn't say a word.

"Where've you been keeping yourself?" the gnome asked, then sucked from his mask.

"What do you want, Gummy?" Blackie didn't offer to shake hands, and the snitch didn't seem to expect it. Instead he smiled a lecherous smile at me.

"Aren't you going to introduce me to your girlfriend?"

Blackie glanced at me, and when I nodded, he said,

"Old Gum used to work Golden Gate Fields, exercise boy. He used to supplement that by selling information." The gnome's gap-toothed grin faded. "Gum, this is Ronnie Ventana."

Gum recovered from Blackie's introduction and offered me a gnarled paw. "Robert C. Purdue," he said with a weak flourish. "It's a real honor to see Blackie's got himself a lady." The way he eyed my low neckline made me glad he wasn't any taller. "Me and Blackie go back a long way. He saved my life, didn't you, Blackie?"

Blackie snorted. "I got you busted, if that's what you're talking about."

Gummy started to laugh, but choked instead. His scrawny body shook with a rattling cough, and his face turned blue. He motioned to his back, so I slapped him a few times, gently between his shoulder blades, while he gasped and wheezed. Then suddenly he seemed to breathe easier.

"Maybe you'd better sit down." I tried to lead him to an empty chair, but he shook me off.

"I'm fine, I'm fine," he panted, then coughed a couple of more times, took a few more pulls from his oxygen mask, and seemed to recover.

Blackie watched him like he would a cockroach.

"Like I was saying, old Blackie here saved my life. If it wasn't for him, I wouldn't be standing here today. He got me off the streets right in time. And things were cooled down enough to where I didn't have to worry once I got out."

"When did you turn P.I.?" Blackie asked skeptically.

Gummy chuckled, showing broken teeth and yellow gums. "Never did. See this card?" He pulled a grimy AIA membership card from his frayed shirt pocket. "I bought it off some guy on Mission Street. Said it was good for a free meal once a month, all year."

So much for exclusivity. Blackie looked disgusted and took my elbow.

"Come on, Ventana. Let's go."

Gummy was undiscouraged. "Nice to see you again, Blackie. I guess we'll be seeing each other next month. You take care of yourself. And your lady too."

As we reached the door, I stole a glance over my shoulder. The speaker was behind the podium now. I couldn't hear a word he was saying, but I could see him clearly. What I saw made me freeze. Blackhand nudged me.

"Come on, doll."

"Look," I said, and pointed at the man on the speaker's dais. He was built as big as a house, with thick black hair. The shock of white at the left temple gleamed under the spotlights.

"That's August," Blackie said. "Change your mind?"

"It's him," I whispered.

"Who?"

"The man I saw this morning. The Fort Point murderer."

Blackie followed my gaze again to the man at the front of the room. "August?" he asked incredulously.

I nodded. "Pete August."

5

"**N**o way, doll."

"It's him, Blackie." When Blackie didn't respond, I said, "Not good, huh?"

"Let me put it this way: I'm probably the only man in this city who'll buy it. That guy's on everybody's A-list."

"See any cops around?" I craned my neck to see if I recognized anybody. Since I only knew three policemen by sight, I wasn't surprised not to recognize any. "Come on," I said, and yanked Blackie out the door.

"Where're we going?"

"The Hall of Justice. He's not going anywhere. If he thought he was in trouble, he wouldn't be here."

As we left the underground parking lot, Blackie lit another cigarette, then pointed his old Buick toward Bryant Street.

"Who do you know down there?" he asked, flicking invisible ash out the window.

"On the police force? Aldo Stivick."

"What the hell's an Aldo Stivick?"

"You say that every time. Mitchell and I went to high school with Aldo. He's almost a sergeant now."

"Homicide?"

"Not exactly."

"What?"

"He's in administration."

Blackie snorted. "Shit, Ventana. You might as well be talkin' to the janitor. What the hell's he going to do for you?"

"Do you know anyone better?"

"You know me and cops don't get on." He dropped ash on his knee while trying to maneuver a right turn. "Why don't you let me handle it?"

"Blackie, you're not a cop. Sometimes you just need a cop. You can't just—"

"Every time I talk to a cop, I get screwed. There's no reason for me to think it's going to be any different for you. I've told you before, the best thing you can do is forget them. Listen to the old teach, will you?" He tossed out his butt and smeared the ash into his pant leg. I tried again.

"Aldo's got access," I said. "Besides, I've *got* to tell them, and Aldo's my best bet."

Blackie shook his head and made a left. "Isn't this the guy you said is hot for you?"

I mumbled something I hoped would sound like yes *and* no. Blackie gave me a knowing look.

"Someday he's going to get tired of you stringing him along. Cops are all the same. You can't trust them, whether they want to get in your pants or not. I never use 'em."

"Blackie, this is a homicide. An open case. They've got to be involved."

"And your Aldo's gonna handle it for you?" He looked

at the clock on his dashboard, which was five hours fast, then at his watch. "Who the hell works administration at nine thirty on a Monday night?"

"Actually Aldo doesn't work at night. I thought I'd call him when we get there and see who he recommends."

Blackie rolled his eyes, then slipped the old Buick into a parking place in front of the Hall. "Were you asleep when I was showing you the ropes?" He lit another smoke. "Look, if you're gonna do this, doll, just take whoever's on duty. That's all your friend's gonna say. Save your twenty cents."

I opened the car door on my side, but he didn't move. "Aren't you coming?"

"You go ahead," he said, and blew smoke out the window.

"Don't be silly, Blackie. Come on."

He shrugged, and we both got out and headed up the steps.

"I bet you get Philly Post," he said as he opened the door for me.

"What's a Philly Post?" I asked. Blackie shot me a withering glance and fell into step with me.

"He's a jerk, that's what he is. He's what your Aldo's gonna be when he grows up."

"Is he in homicide?" Blackie nodded, and a flicker of hope surfaced in my breast. "You mean you know somebody in homicide?"

I was thinking along the lines of a personal introduction. Blackie tossed his half-finished cigarette into the ashcan and walked through the metal detector.

"Yeah."

"That's great! You said you didn't have any contacts down here. You've been holding out on me, you dog."

Aldo was my only, therefore my best, contact in the police department. The other two cops I knew refused to talk to me, much less help. If I could set myself up with Philly Post, who was actually *in* homicide, I'd have a good solid contact who wouldn't have to go through hoops to find out specifics on a case, at least not homicides. I could kiss Aldo and his tight little conscience good-bye. My spirits soared. No more unpleasant little lunches in exchange for information.

"Philly Post can't be all bad," I said. "Will you introduce us?"

"If he's working tonight, you bet," Blackie said, and his chuckle echoed in the empty hallway. "You bet your ass I will."

6

I sat down in front of Philly Post's plain metal desk. A tacky little nameplate, engraved with his proper name and title: *Lieutenant Harold Post,* was Scotch-taped to the front edge of the desk. The windowless office was stark: no lamps, no shelves, just an overhead light, three hard wooden chairs—two in front and one behind the desk—and stacks and stacks of papers and folders on the desk. The air inside the room felt tight and musty and smelled vaguely of dirty socks.

We'd been waiting on those hard little chairs for twenty minutes while Post grunted monosyllabic responses into the phone. He'd taken the call just as we walked in and had pretty much ignored us since.

I studied him while he talked. He was a big, barrel-chested man in his mid-forties with a tough, grizzled face, flat cheekbones and large, even white teeth. Soggy half-moons of sweat darkened the armpits of his shirt, but everything else about him seemed as cool as a shark —like he could have gone either way—con or cop—and happened to pick the right side of the law by accident.

Bushy eyebrows hid most of the expression in his face, but when he saw Blackie, I noticed his eyes turn cold. So what if they weren't on the best of terms, I'd still give him a shot. I stared at the mountain of bureaucratic debris on his desk for a while, then toed a cigarette burn on the scarred linoleum until he hung up.

"Yeah?" The snarl in his voice did not bode well. For a moment I wavered. Was it really best not to say anything? But it was already too late. Blackie was introducing me, just as he'd promised.

Post frowned. "Ventana? . . . Ventana . . . Have we met before?"

"No." I noticed the cuffs and collar of his shirt were frayed.

"Didn't I pop you for something? I know I've heard that name." He glanced at Blackie, who shrugged and fingered his lighter, then smirked at me. I plowed into my story and silently cursed Blackie for enjoying this.

Post's sneer didn't leave his face until I'd finished. Then it dissolved into a mocking mask of condescension. I was starting to think maybe he wouldn't make such a great contact after all.

"Now I got it. You're Cisco Ventana's kid, aren't you? The jewel thieves, him and the society girl he married." He drew himself up in his chair. "You've got a lot of nerve coming in here."

I guess I should have expected it, but I never have been able to develop the thick skin I need to handle all the crap I get over my parents. Funny that they never laid down any boundaries for me when they were alive, but from the grave have managed to circumscribe certain parts of my world quite a bit. Dealing with the law was a big one. I didn't want to be this cop's best friend, but it would have been nice to start out at least with a clean slate.

"I didn't come here to talk about my parents," I told him. "August's the issue here, not them."

"Do you know who Pete August is?"

I held his angry black eyes without blinking. "He's a murder suspect."

"Pete August is a private investigator. One of the best." Something resembling respect crept into Post's voice. "He's a *real* P.I."

I let that one go. Blackhand shuffled his feet in the chair next to mine and flashed me an I-told-you-so look. "Detective Post, I saw him throttle a man and drown him. I'm an eyewitness."

Post's smile was sour. "In the first place Pete August wouldn't whack anybody. I want that clear right now. That's point one. And point two is if he *was* going to whack somebody, he wouldn't do it in broad daylight in front of a witness. You don't know what you're talking about. Where's the body? Got any corroboration?"

I held on to what little patience I had left. "I explained all that. The Coast Guard's still looking. And as for corroboration, since when do you need *two* witnesses? Just check the report."

"I haven't seen one."

I glanced meaningfully at the chaos on his desk. "Have you tried checking one of those piles?"

He shot me an impatient look and pushed himself out of his chair, then paced back and forth behind his desk. In his sweat-stained shirt he looked like the "before" picture in a deodorant ad. "What we've got is—"

Somebody rapped on the glass door behind me. A pot-bellied old Chinese woman stood poised outside the half-opened door, mop and dustrag in hand. Post should have

welcomed her with open arms, but instead he wagged a
finger at her and raised his voice like people do when they
know the person they're talking to can't understand a
word they're saying. "NOT TONIGHT," he shouted.
"TOMORROW. Come back TOMORROW."

The woman shook her head in disgust, shut the door,
then waddled around the corner. I turned back to Post in
time to see him lodge the frown back on his face.

"Still looking," he snapped. "No body. No report. No
record of anything going down." He glanced at Blackie,
then back at me. "You know what I think?" He paused
for emphasis, not because he expected an answer. "I
think you're full of—"

"Lieutenant Post—" Mentally I cursed him. Then I
cursed Officer Tucker, the military police in general, and
government agencies as a whole. I even cursed Blackie
again when, out of the corner of my eye, I saw his face
twitch in amusement. He really was enjoying this.

"Look," I said, working to keep the anger out of my
voice. "I know what I saw. Just because the paperwork
hasn't come through doesn't mean it didn't happen. Just
because you think August is a real stand-up guy doesn't
mean he couldn't commit a murder."

The bushy brows settled over unreadable eyes, and I
wondered if Philly Post was this rude all the time. Maybe
it was just a bad day for him. Maybe his cat died or his
wife yelled at him before he came to work. I tried again.

"With all due respect—"

"With all due respect," he repeated sourly. "What?"

Beside me Blackie coughed. I ignored him and met
Post's hot black eyes.

"When you find the report and decide to look into it,"
I said, "you've got a witness. I'd like to go on record
tonight."

Philly Post sighed, collapsed into his chair, and pressed a button on a tiny intercom buried under the untidy mess on his desk.

"Get in here," he barked at the poor whomever on the other end. Then to me, "You could have made a mistake."

"I make mistakes all the time," I said slowly. "But I didn't this time."

He scowled at the skinny young man in uniform who appeared at the door. Philly came around his desk. Close up, he was even more intimidating, and he seemed to know it too.

"Take a statement from her, Kendall."

I glanced across at Blackhand, then back at the officer hovering obsequiously behind me. Then I stood, and Blackie did too.

No way was Philly Post going to be any easy contact to cultivate. In fact I wasn't even sure I ever wanted to see him again. I cast one last look at his rumpled, frowning face, wished he'd been somebody—anybody—else, and walked out.

7

As tempted as I was to keep on going, I didn't. It was important to get my statement on record. That took only fifteen minutes. After I'd spent two hours with Officer Tucker that morning, Kendall seemed the model of efficiency. When it was over, I felt better. I'd done my civic duty, no thanks to Philly Post.

"He likes you," Blackie said in the elevator on the way down.

"Post? Are you crazy? He chewed me up and spit me out."

Blackie grinned. "He didn't throw you out."

I laughed out loud. "He *had* to talk to me. He *had* to take a statement."

"That's where you're wrong. Philly Post doesn't have to do anything he doesn't want to. Right now he likes you. He still might, once he figures out the Ventana jewel heists were your folks, not you. Just make sure he doesn't find out about your hobby."

"Why? He's in homicide, not burglary."

"Doll, if he finds out you bust alarms for kicks, he'll

nail you no matter what detail he works. The man's a law machine, just like all the rest. Shit for brains."

The elevator doors opened, and Blackie reached for another cigarette. I bounced out, dodging a Vietnamese janitor slinging a mop, while Blackie hung behind lighting his smoke.

"You know, I feel lucky to get out of there alive." I stopped by the pay phone at the end of the hall. "Wait up a minute, will you? I'm going to call Aldo."

Blackie took a long drag, exhaled, then scowled. "Why?"

"He's still my only police contact." I slipped inside the booth before he could talk me out of it. The phone rang eight times before somebody finally picked it up. "Aldo? Did I wake you up?"

"Who is this? Ronnie?" His groggy voice lacked its normal primness.

"Were you sleeping?"

"I was watching the game."

"Uh, listen, Aldo. I'm sorry to interrupt but I need some information about a private investigator. His name's Pete August. Do you think you can get something for me tomorrow?"

Suddenly he sounded wide awake. "Probably. If I can, I'll have it by noon. Want to meet then?"

I sighed out loud. Lunch. His pound of flesh. "Where?"

"I'll meet you at the Venus Café," he said, then, as if he'd just thought of it, he added, "We can have lunch."

I rolled my eyes, told him I'd be there, and hung up. When I came out of the booth, I collided with a uniformed cop escorting a sobbing black woman out of the elevator.

"Sorry," I said, but they didn't even notice me. Her

sobs faded to whimpers as they retreated down the deserted hall. A phone rang behind the bullet-proof glass at the end of the lobby, and the cop behind the desk picked it up. I looked for Blackie and found him around the corner, just inside the front doors, talking to a slim, well-dressed brunette in her early forties. Blackie introduced the woman as Judge Martha Coyle.

"I testified in her court a couple of times," he explained.

The handsome woman in front of me, still flushed from whatever roguish remark Blackie had just made, had straight hair pulled off her face and tied in a neat chignon. Her gray slacks and the suede jacket she wore over a frilly blouse looked expensive, maybe hand-tailored. With her proud carriage, high cheekbones, and full lips, she looked more like a model than an officer of the court, but her briefcase overflowed with transcripts and scribbled-up yellow legal pads. When she spoke, her voice was deep and smooth and confident.

"I understand you've had quite an adventure today," she said to me.

I smiled ruefully. "That's one way to put it."

"Judge Coyle put away the Russian Hill rapist a couple of years back. Remember that?"

The trial had been in the papers every day for months. One of the victims had been everybody's favorite socialite, a nice lady who couldn't dance anymore, or even walk. She'd been reduced to a quadriplegic from the rapist's attack.

"That must have been rough," I said, thinking of having to sit through all the gruesome testimony and stay impartial enough to make a judgment.

"It was."

"What'd you give him, Judge?" Blackie asked. "A hundred years?"

Martha Coyle's face went rigid. "That's what he should have gotten," she said. "He deserved more than that."

"I guess the law's got upper limits," I said mildly.

"Exactly. Sometimes the system—" She broke off, and shook her head. "I'd better save the lecture. Words don't serve any purpose. If I go into it, we'll be here all night." While she spoke, her eyes drifted back to Blackie and her face softened. "There are more pleasant things in the world," she said.

Blackie winked at her. "You got that right, Judge."

She flirted with him for a couple of minutes more while I watched, intrigued that a judge was as susceptible to Blackie's charm as every other woman in the world.

"You're welcome to come back and testify anytime," she told him warmly, then said good-bye and disappeared down the hall. Blackie watched her go with a grin on his face, then caught my eye.

"What are you lookin' at?" he asked.

"She's a neat lady."

Blackie looked pleased. "For a judge she's a real looker." His smile could have been from a memory or just from the pleasure of seeing such a pretty woman. I bagged my curiosity. I'd ask him about her some other time. Blackie started toward the door. "So what's your friend say?"

"He's going to check August out for me. If they've got anything on record, he should be able to turn it up."

"Yeah?" He sounded skeptical. "You going to back-burn it till tomorrow?"

"I haven't got much choice."

"Great. Let's forget this shit. Joey's playing down at the Dock. Want to check it out?"

I glanced at my watch. It was late, but when I thought of the two empty rooms waiting for me at home and the long night that stretched ahead, I slipped my arm through Blackie's and led him out the door.

"First round's on me," I said.

8

Blackie's son, Joey, played until closing, then invited everyone who was still ambulatory over to his place in the East Bay. He played his trumpet for a couple of hours more, until about four in the morning, jazz mostly, with some blues mixed in, the kind of melancholy, soulful music I love to hear. I was impressed. He was good, bound to be a star someday. But first he had to pay his dues. They all did.

And I felt as though I'd paid mine when I dragged myself out of bed the next morning. The clock said eleven but it seemed like dawn, and I felt like the living dead. Too much blues and too much booze. My legs were like lead.

No run today. I had to meet Aldo at noon anyway. Christ! The Venus Café. I shuddered, put on the Mr. Coffee and headed for the shower.

An hour later, dressed in slacks, low-heeled shoes, and a jacket over my sweater, I waited for Aldo, squinting into the sun outside the Venus Café.

The place was one of those quiet neighborhood restaurants that are kept open by a handful of faithful customers but are too poor to make any improvements. Even their burglar alarm system was low-style—a no-challenge local alarm with a bell box nailed above the front door. Nothing that couldn't be handled with lock picks, wire clippers, and a can of shaving cream.

As Aldo approached from down the block, decked out in his navy-blue jumpsuit, pressed and decorated with badge and arm patches, I wondered what went through his head every morning when he put on all that regalia just to sit behind a desk all day. He wasn't bad-looking—or good-looking, either, come to think of it. He had a weak chin and thinning brown hair, a light build, and undistinguished features that fit about seventy-five percent of the male populace. He was so average he could rob a bank without a mask and they'd never be able to describe him with any kind of accuracy. Nothing stood out about his personality, either, except maybe that he took his job way too seriously. Back in the sixties you could have called him uptight.

"Sorry I'm late," he said when he came up to me. He was bristling with self-importance. "I had to issue a citation on my way over. Jaywalker."

"Hope you weren't too tough on him," I said.

"Oh, no. I just—" He broke off, suddenly uncertain.

"I'm just teasing, Aldo."

He forced a chuckle. "Yeah, heh, heh."

We got a seat in a corner by the front window. Sunshine streamed in on us, warming my aching back and illuminating Aldo's pale face. That's what came of office work.

"What a table, heh? We really lucked out, didn't we?" Aldo said.

I didn't have the heart to tell him I would have preferred the dark one in the back or one in the basement, even, if they had one. I managed a smile for the waitress, who buzzed up milliseconds after we sat down to chirp her name and the specials of the day.

"Bring me a Bloody Mary," I said as soon as she finished. Hair of the dog. It was the only way to join the living.

Aldo glanced pointedly at his watch, but I wasn't going to go for it today.

"Why don't you have one too?" I said cheerfully.

"I can't. I'm on duty."

"Do you ever? Drink, I mean?"

He lifted his napkin out from under his silverware, unfolded it, and slipped it under the table. "I have a beer every now and then."

"Like when you're watching a game or something?"

"Exactly." He lined up his knife, spoon, and fork all in a row beside his plate.

"That's good, Aldo."

The Bloody Mary arrived and I sipped while Aldo pretended not to disapprove. He ducked his head behind the menu for a while, so I killed time by checking out the alarm wires. They ran from the bell box around the side wall to the back. The control box was probably in the kitchen.

"The avocado omelets here are good," Aldo said. "I can recommend the Viennese salad too. Black olives and anchovies."

My stomach lurched, and I choked on my drink.

"Are you all right, Ronnie? Here, have some water."

I sputtered into my napkin and shook my head. "No, no, please. I'm fine." When the waitress came for our order, I asked for a turkey sandwich.

Aldo shifted in his chair and looked disappointed.

"You're sure? They import their anchovies, you know. And the—"

I raised my hand. "All right. Change mine to the omelet." I'd have to force myself to eat it, but at least Aldo might be more forthcoming if he thought I was like him. Before the waitress left, I drained my Bloody Mary and asked for another.

"Did you get anything?" I asked when she'd left. I'd waited what I considered a decent interval.

Aldo looked blank.

"Pete August, remember?"

"Oh, yes." He looked guilty but kept on talking. It didn't make sense that his conscience bothered him. It was his choice; he was the one who offered to feed me information in the first place. "He's got no priors. He's a private investigator. Did you know that?"

"Yeah."

"His office is in the SP Building. Not the one at the foot of Market but the one over on Third by Townsend. He lives in Marin."

I knew that much from the phone book. "Does he have any partners? Anybody working for him?"

"I don't think so."

"Has he ever been in any kind of trouble?"

"Not that I know of."

Aldo wasn't exactly blowing me away with the inside scoop on August. I decided to stick to the little stuff. "Is he married?"

"No."

"What about his car? What kind of car does he own?"

"A black BMW."

The second Bloody Mary arrived, and I sipped it more slowly than the first. "Anything else?"

"He used to work for the D.A.'s office and before that he was on the force for a while."

I set my glass down carefully. "So he's got friends in both places."

"I guess, if he made a good impression."

"Is there any way you could find out what he's working on?"

Aldo regarded me with open curiosity. "What's this all about?"

This was part of the trade. I debated whether to lie or not and opted for the truth. Aldo should be able to handle it, he was a big boy.

"I saw him kill somebody," I said, and watched every line on Aldo's nondescript face screw up into a solid mask of horror. He tried to speak, but all he could manage were short sputters. Finally he got it out.

"What did you say? It's—it's a homicide?"

"It happened yesterday."

"Dammit, Ronnie!" He looked around the room like he expected to be handcuffed and led away right then and there. "Excuse the language, but you should know better. You can't investigate an open homicide. You *know* that. I can't get involved in one either." He shook his head. "You can't go near them, Ronnie."

"There's no law against it. Homicide just doesn't like to share."

The waitress appeared with our omelets, and he waited, silently fuming, while she served them. I stared with loathing at the plate in front of me. The omelet was runny.

As soon as she left, Aldo exploded. "Did you at least report it?" he hissed.

"Of course I did. In fact Lieutenant Post and I had a nice little chat about it last night."

Aldo looked like he wanted to cry. "Not Philly Post! He'll kill me if he finds out."

I studied Aldo's forehead, waiting for little beads of sweat to pop out. Next time I'd lie.

"Don't worry. I don't think Post would care. He doesn't believe me anyway."

Right away I knew I'd said the wrong thing. Aldo drew himself up and pressed his lips together. "An officer's job is not to believe or disbelieve, Ronnie. He just takes down the information and investigates for the truth."

It sounded straight out of a fifties cop show. Aldo had been on desk duty too long.

"Did he take down your statement?" he asked miserably.

"Yeah, he did." I almost said I'd forced him to, but Aldo seemed to be just getting over his peeve. Why rock the boat?

"See? You really have the wrong idea about police officers. We're just in it to help the public. People keep getting the wrong idea about us."

He seemed satisfied to lecture me on the public's misperceptions about the altruistic nature of cops. The way Aldo painted it, the SFPD was just one big Boy Scout troop out to save the world.

I picked up my fork and cut a corner off the omelet, away from the runny center. I closed my eyes, pushed the fork resolutely into my mouth, and chewed.

"Omelet's great, Aldo. Delicious." I opened my eyes and found his eager ones on mine.

"Is it?" He shoved a load of egg into his mouth, set his fork down while he chewed, and seemed to forget our little tiff. I took another bite and smiled across the table at him.

"Do you think you can ask around and see what he's working on?"

He started to shake his head, but I caught his eye and winked at him before he could say no.

"Please?" I wasn't above begging.

"Dammit, Ronnie. Excuse the language, but I could get in big trouble."

"It's just a one-time thing, Aldo."

He frowned and picked up his fork again. "I don't know, Ronnie. Let me think about it, okay? Give me some time to think about it and we can talk again."

Damn. Another lunch.

9

I drove down to the Hall of Justice. Instead of going straight to Post's office, I stopped at the front desk and asked who was handling the Fort Point murder case on the off-chance it had been assigned to somebody else.

"I don't know," the cute young hunk behind the desk said. "Let me see."

The room behind the bullet-proof glass was a different world from the deserted vacuum of the night before. Phones were ringing, people were talking, some were shouting, and about five men stared at me with undisguised curiosity from beside a water cooler in the back. The hunk shuffled through the notebook on his desk, then turned his back to me.

"Hey, Lieutenant! Who's got that Fort Point case?"

"Who wants to know?" The unmistakable pearly whites and bushy eyebrows emerged from behind a file cabinet beside the desk. "Oh." Philly Post's expression told me he wasn't happy to see me, but he couldn't possibly have been as disappointed as I was to see him.

"Yeah?" he said by way of inquiry. He had on a different shirt, and the sleeves were rolled up, but it was pitted out as bad as the one he'd worn last night.

I looked through the glass at the bustling room and the expectant faces inside. Most of the previous bustle had ceased. I'd suddenly become the center of attention.

"Can we talk in your office?"

Post shrugged, motioned toward the door, then buzzed me in and told me to come upstairs. I followed him to his office. The stacks of folders on his desk seemed to have multiplied during the night. I closed the door behind me and sat down. He cleared a corner and perched his hip on the edge of his desk, then fixed me with an ugly stare.

"What do you want?"

"I was in the neighborhood," I began. "I wanted to make sure you got Sergeant Tucker's report. Did he send it over?"

He stared at me a long time, probably contemplating whether to answer me or just tell me to go to hell. "I got it."

"Were you able to arrest August?"

He unclipped his I.D. badge from his shirt collar and held it out to me. "You want my job? Here." He dangled the laminated card in my face. "Take it."

"I don't want your job, Lieutenant Post. I'm just concerned. This guy's a murderer and I'm the only witness who can put him at Fort Point."

"We're taking care of it."

"I'm sure you are."

He tossed the I.D. on top of the papers on his desk, and I wondered if he'd ever be able to find it again.

"Unless you've got something new to add—" he said.

"Do you mind if I talk to him?"

He scowled. "Talk to who?"

"August. I'd like to see him."

"Christ!" He pushed himself off the desk, circled behind it, and slouched into his chair. "You've got a problem, you know that?"

I was getting the message. "You haven't arrested him, have you?"

"We talked to him, all right? He said he didn't do it." He raised a hand to silence my protest. "He's got an alibi."

"He can't! I saw—"

"Whatever you saw, *Ms.* Ventana, it wasn't Pete August dunking some jerk in the Bay."

I traced a worn groove in the arm of the chair with the edge of my fingernail and counted to ten, then raised my eyes to meet Post's. "Do you know August? You've met him, haven't you?"

He didn't even blink. "I know him, sure. So does half the force. You got a problem with that?"

"I thought *you* might," I said.

"I don't know what makes you think you can yank me around, Ventana. I had you checked out, you know. For a P.I. you sure have a weird hobby. I guess your parents showed you the ropes."

"My parents? Sure, they taught me a lot of things to help me out in life. Like right now for instance. My father said Americans are never as polite as Mexicans. And my mother, even though she was Anglo, agreed. They told me I should always hark back to my Mexican heritage and be polite no matter what. Even if somebody treats me rotten, I should always give the person the benefit of the doubt. Maybe that person doesn't know any better, they said. Maybe that person lacks education, or just plain good manners. Whatever the reason, they told me, I shouldn't use that person's lack of civility as an excuse for my own."

Post scowled. "Don't give me that shit. They were burglars. You know it and I know—"

"Alleged," I said.

"What?"

"They died before they went to trial."

"Yeah, right. That's just a technicality. The way I hear it, the department had 'em cold. You know, one of these days somebody's going to press charges against you. They're not going to fall for that 'I-was-just-testing-your-alarm-system-and-boy-does-it-need-work' crap. One of these days they're not going to fall all over themselves to pay you to design a new setup for them." He shook his finger at me. "And when that happens, Burglary's going to have special instructions to call me. I want to see you go down. I want to see you lose that license."

I turned my most guileless expression on him. "Oh, really. Why?"

"Because you're giving me a headache, *Ms.* Ventana." He pointed at the bustling men outside his office. "See those guys out there? They're bustin' their butts to get the job done. I've got two times the caseload I ought to have for the men I've got. Most days I don't get home until midnight, and you want me to drop everything to chase this little piece of garbage you've handed me. If you really want to help, why don't you make restitution for all that shit your parents ripped off?" He circled the desk and opened the door. Chatter from the squad room rushed in at us. Through gritted teeth, he said, "I've got work to do. Good-bye, *Ms.* Ventana."

I fumed all the way to the car. There was no excuse for Post's Neanderthal behavior. If my parents had lived to meet him, they probably would have revoked their "be genteel and polite" rule.

No way around it: Post was a jerk, just like Blackie

said he was, and it was pretty clear he wasn't going to do much of anything.

Without really thinking, I drove over to the Third and Townsend address Aldo had given me. As I circled the block, I wondered who had given August his alibi. I'd have to ask Aldo—somehow—to look into it. As long as I didn't try to change his view of the big picture, where a big fat line ran right down the middle between right and wrong, Aldo could be persuaded to sin occasionally—in little bits.

I circled the block, then parked the car across the street, half a block down from a squat three-story renovated office building. In bronze, across massive double oak doors, was the number 311. A distinct red plaque in the corner told me that Noman Security protected the premises. August's office was inside.

From where I sat, I could see the front half of the building's nearly empty parking lot. It looked like there was only one exit to the lot and I was looking at it. Three cars, all expensive, lined the front row, but the one that caught my eye was the top-of-the-line black BMW closest to me.

I settled in to wait and watch, wondering what kind of security Noman used and if they had a guard inside. A second later a tap on my window made me gasp. I'd been so intent on watching the building I hadn't even noticed the police car behind me. I was getting sloppy. I rolled down my window.

"Excuse me, miss," the officer said. "I'm going to have to ask you to move along."

"Is this a No Parking zone?" I craned my neck to read the street-cleaning sign on the light post a couple of cars down. It said, No Parking Thurs 4–7 A.M. Even if he could convince me it was Thursday instead of Tuesday, I knew it was after noon. I read the policeman's name tag and smiled. "What's the problem, Officer Ryan?"

The patrolman smiled back at me, but it wasn't a friendly smile. "We can't have any loitering around here." He dropped his face down even with mine, and his expression turned ominous. "I'm going to have to ask you to move along. Drive careful, now. I'd hate to have to issue you a citation."

Damn! Understaffed, my eye. Busting their butts. Sure! If I'd had any doubts that August had connections, they were gone now. Officer Ryan ambled back to his car and waited for me to pull out. I circled around a couple of times, but he stayed right on my tail.

Damn. He followed me to the underground garage of the Embarcadero Center, parked a few rows down from where I did, and waved to me as I packed a grocery bag full of junk from the backseat and headed for the elevators. Ten minutes later I took Mitch's Citroën and left Officer Ryan guarding my Toyota on the next floor down.

The black BMW was still in the lot on Third and Townsend when I drove up thirty minutes later. Presumably August was still inside the building. Waiting, subconsciously ticking off the minutes in my head, I watched. I was good at this. It was slow and boring, but sometimes I actually enjoyed it.

10

When a tall figure lumbered out of the building an hour later, I sat up in my seat. August got into his black BMW, revved it up, then headed toward the freeway. I followed him across the Bay Bridge, down Highway 17, then off the Fourteenth Street exit to a shabby industrial section in Oakland. It was a desolate part of town, made up mostly of abandoned warehouses, railyards, and broken-down boxcars.

A blue station wagon swept down the ramp in front of me, stopped at the foot of the slope, then turned left. I edged the Citroën into the intersection behind it, then scanned the deserted streets on either side of me. There was no sign of the BMW, but the car behind me honked, so I turned right, dodging foot-wide potholes and rubble as I drove to the first warehouse on my right. I stopped at the mouth of a little alley and looked down it. Still no BMW. But something down there moved, a flash in the late-afternoon sun. I started to duck down in the seat, then relaxed. It was just a wino wandering amid the sunless shadows and empty docks.

I edged the car forward another block before I finally saw it. The black sedan was parked around the corner, almost hidden behind a boarded-up building and the decaying remains of a loading dock.

I backed the Citroën out of sight behind a dumpster across the street and left it there. Then I edged my way forward, hugging the crumbling loading dock for cover as I closed in on the yawning black hole that was the door.

Seven worm-eaten wooden steps at the far end led from street level, where I stood, up to the loading dock. From there five paces would take me to the door.

A couple of yards from the steps I set my hands on the rotted wooden planks of the dock to boost myself up, but stopped when I heard voices coming toward me from inside the warehouse. I dropped back onto the ground and crouched beside the dock, searching for a place to hide. Two short steps away, under the stairs, was a half-opened hatch. I scrambled for it and slipped inside just as footsteps clattered onto the dock floor over my head.

The crawl space went the length of the dock and reeked of decay and excrement. It was filled with trash and gravel and probably every species of roach and spider invented. Every time I moved, I stirred up little clouds of dust. I blinked and listened hard. The voices were muffled overhead, then silent. The footsteps stopped right over my head. I strained to hear words, but all I heard was some kind of sniffing and rasping behind me. *What the hell?* I crooked my neck over my shoulder and saw movement in the semidarkness behind me.

Rats. Rats as big as dogs. "Shit," I muttered, and counted their gleaming little eyes. Six eyes, three rats. The closest one was about five feet away, scratching around in the trash looking for God-only-knew-what.

The other two were mere shadows. In the dark I couldn't make out much beyond their shapes, but to me they all looked famished. I kept my eyes on them and they kept theirs on me as I slowly started backing away. The top of my head scraped the under part of the dock. *Damn.*

"What's that?" a voice above me asked. I held my breath and waited.

"It's only rats. They're not going to eat you," a second voice said.

I peered up through a crack in the floorboards and found myself eye-to-eye with the flat, broad face of Pete August. He was standing over me, staring straight down between his feet, his face probably six feet away from mine. I froze and my mouth went dry.

August scraped his foot along the crack in the floorboard, shifting dust and sand through the slit. The stuff fell all over my head and into my eyes. *Shit.* Now I was cornered *and* blinded. I waited for him to shout or yell or something while I blinked frantically to get the dirt out of my eyes. But he just kept on talking, and I realized that with the play of sunlight above and the shadows below he couldn't see me. My nose started to run.

"Do you understand what I want?" August asked. The rats made a kind of mewing sound behind me. I checked over my shoulder. The big one was closer now—about four feet away. I scooted nearer the little door and tried to make up my mind which would hurt me less: the animal rats down here or the human rats above.

"Yeah, yeah. Sure. I gotcha, Mr. A. No problem." The second voice sounded sort of wheezing and familiar. The footsteps traveled along the dock, then down the wooden stairs. I followed the sound with my eyes but stayed back in the shadows, creeping forward just far enough to see out the partially closed hatch door.

The second man came into view. His back I'd seen before, and the green canister under his arm pretty much gave him away. Then he turned his face, and I gave myself a big fat pat on the back: Robert C. Purdue— Gummy—or, as Blackie referred to him, the "little snitch."

What was the classiest P.I. in town doing with a sleazy little snitch like Purdue?

"You got a deal, Mr. A. You won't regret it." Purdue offered August his hand, but the look on August's face could have frozen lava. He made a gesture, sort of like shooing away a cur, and Purdue scurried out of sight. He moved just like the rats behind me, quick and sniffing, his nose figuratively to the ground. I followed the sound of his feet as he went up the steps and back into the building.

August disappeared from my sight, and while I listened for his car, I checked for the rats again. This time five pairs of eyes gleamed at me from the dark. I bit down hard on my lip so that I wouldn't scream and watched them creep forward, moving toward me in a small army like some kind of synchronized rat patrol. I checked the little bit of space around me and grabbed the first thing I saw—an old broom handle somebody had chucked under there probably a thousand years ago. When they saw me pick it up and wave it at them, they hesitated, then started forward again. Shit.

In the distance, finally, thankfully, I heard an engine start—a smooth, high-tech turbo sort of sound. It had to be August's BMW.

"Hurry, damn you," I muttered, then jabbed the biggest of the rats and swung the stick at the others. They snarled, jumped, and scratched the air, but held their ground. I jabbed again and heard the satisfying *thunk* as it connected with something living.

The sound of August's engine faded into the distance. Just as the rats started forward again, I gave them one last jab of the pole and scrambled out the hatch, gasping for air and light.

An engine coughed to life somewhere behind the warehouse. Pulling myself to my feet, I ran to the Citroën. When I caught up with Gummy Purdue, he was coaxing a filthy old Chevy out of the next alley down.

I trailed him to a crumbling apartment building in downtown Oakland, on Jefferson by the highway, and parked right out in front. Purdue wouldn't be expecting me. He didn't strike me as the kind of person who'd survived because he was careful, just lucky.

When I checked the mailboxes, his name was listed under number 208. The front door to the building had a lock, but it was broken so I just walked up to the second floor and knocked.

"Who's there?"

"It's Ronnie Ventana. We met last night, remember? I'm a friend of Blackie's."

The door rattled as he unfastened the latch and opened it a crack. As soon as he saw me, he recognized me and opened the door wide, treating me to the same lecherous grin I'd seen the night before. "What a surprise!" he cackled. "What a surprise!" His green air canister was nowhere in sight.

"Have you got a minute? I want to talk to you about Pete August."

He was quick, but not quick enough. I stuck my foot in the crack just before he could slam the door shut.

"Ouch!" For a scrawny old man he was doing a fairly good job crushing my toes. I jammed my shoulder against the door and shoved. It wasn't a nice thing to do, but he didn't give me a choice.

After a minute a death-rattle gasp sounded from behind the door. The tension against my shoulder eased, and the door suddenly fell open to a winded Purdue, scrabbling frantically for the clear plastic mask and green canister on a table in the center of the room. He cranked the valve on the tank wide open, smashed the mask over his face, and sucked for all he was worth.

I went in, took his arm, and led him to the only chair in the room. "Are you all right, Mr. Purdue?"

He collapsed into the seat, took a couple more tokes, then lifted the mask and nodded.

"Uh—ugh!" He gasped, then breathed from the mask again. His chest sounded like a swamp.

I closed the door and scanned the sparsely furnished apartment. It made mine look like a penthouse suite: one chair, the table, a hot plate, and a rumpled mattress on the floor—just a blanket, no sheets—in the corner. The paint on the walls was peeling, the single tarnished window was without curtains, and the whole place reeked of stale booze and vomit. Not exactly the Ritz. I waited for him to catch his breath.

"I'm sorry I had to do that, Mr. Purdue. Are you going to be all right?"

His color was back, and when he nodded this time, I believed him.

"I need to know what you and August talked about," I said.

His liquid eyes, suspicious and alert, were like a cornered weasel's. Suddenly he didn't look like a decrepit old lech anymore. He looked sharp and sinister.

"Who'd you say?"

"I saw you over at the railyards."

He didn't say anything. He just sat there sucking deep breaths from the canister. I wondered how much better his health might be if he didn't have to breathe the disgusting smell inside the apartment. I crossed to the grimy window and tried to open it, but it was painted shut. I looked out. A bag lady methodically rummaged through the garbage cans lined up across the street.

"So what'd he want?" I asked softly.

The repulsive sucking behind me stopped. "He just asked me about some shit."

"What shit?"

"You know, mutual acquaintances, shit like that."

I turned in time to see him press his dry, withered lips together stubbornly. I understood. His sagging eyes sparkled when I pulled a five-dollar bill from my pocket and held it up. Probably half a month's rent.

"Anybody in particular?" I asked.

"Lon Wilson."

"Who's he?"

"A bum."

I took a step toward him, but he started to choke and raised the oxygen mask to his face again. This time he didn't sound so bad, and when I pulled out another bill, he stopped coughing immediately and lowered the mask.

"He wanted to know where to find him."

"What did you tell him?"

"I said I didn't know. I'd have to ask around." He showed his gap-toothed smile. "It's no good to put out the first time around."

I folded the two bills lengthwise and ran the crease between my thumb and forefinger. "What does August want with Wilson?"

"I figure he's got a job for him. Why else would he ask?"

"What's this Lonnie Wilson into?"

"Anything that pays," Gummy said promptly. "He'll do anything for the money."

"And August knows that?"

"Everybody does." Purdue was starting to loosen up. "I told him I'd put the word out that he needs to see him, but he said no, just find him. That's all. Don't talk to him."

"Do you work for August a lot?"

"Looks like I'm gonna. I told him about my services the other night, last night, you know, at that detective thing. To tell you the truth, I was kind of surprised to see him go for it so fast." His eyes wandered to the bills in my hand. "Truth is, I'm surprised to see you too."

I pulled out a ten and tossed all three bills on the table, then laid my card on top of them.

"Call me before you call him," I said. "And let's keep this confidential."

He dropped his mask and grabbed the cash, letting the oxygen hiss into the open room. Only after he'd stuffed the money into his shirt pocket did he lock the valve on the tank and set the gear on the floor beside him.

"Sure thing," he said, and followed me to the door with his drooping red-rimmed eyes. "I'll be in touch."

11

I stopped at the first pay phone I saw and looked up Lon Wilson in the phone book. He probably wasn't listed, but it wouldn't hurt to check.

The Oakland Wilsons went from LeRoy to Lo Tan. No Lon. Directory Assistance had nothing on him, either, so I called Aldo and listened for seven minutes while he explained that he'd searched his soul and just couldn't bring himself to help me with August anymore. It was an open homicide investigation, he had his career to consider, and he just couldn't do it.

If he was angling for another lunch, it just wasn't going to happen. I had to draw the line somewhere. I'd had lunch with him once this week already.

"I understand," I told him.

"You do?" Aldo sounded surprised, not relieved. To me that only confirmed that he'd been after another meal together. It was good the SFPD kept him in administration. He was too transparent. On the streets the man would be a sitting duck.

"Sure, Aldo. No problem. But something else has

come up. Can you check it out for me? Don't worry. I won't ask you to look up August again," I said firmly, trying to ignore the stab at my conscience.

"Well . . . I . . ."

"I only need to know what you've got on a Lon Wilson. L-O-N W-I-L-S-O-N. I don't have a DOB or DMV, but I'm pretty sure he's got a record. Can you punch his name in real quick and tell me where he lives? I'm at a pay phone in Oakland."

"I'm not at my desk, Ronnie. Sorry. How about—?"

If he thought he was going to parlay this scrap into a discussion over another lunch, he was dead wrong. Best to head him off at the pass.

"I'll call you back in fifteen minutes. Will that give you enough time?"

"Well, I—"

"Great! Talk to you then."

I hung up. No point in going back to the city until I knew where Wilson lived. He could be in the East Bay, and I'd only have to come right back if I went home. Just to kill some time, I phoned my answering machine and played back my messages. The first was from Edna Burrows at the Oakland Parole Office, asking me to phone when I had a chance. We'd kept in touch after I quit. There were two calls from Aldo—I'd already cleared that up with him—and one from Mitchell telling me what a mistake I was making by not talking to Skip about the job. I counted my dimes and called Edna.

"You haven't forgotten Dirty Harry's retirement party, have you?" Edna asked. Harry was the old patriarch of the parole office. He'd been there since time immemorial.

"It's on my calendar," I said. "Tomorrow. One o'clock at the office, right?"

"That's it."

"I'll be there," I assured her. "While I've got you on the phone, can you check something out for me?"

"Sure. What's his name?"

I laughed. "I guess you've got my number." Edna couldn't find Lon Wilson in the system. That only meant he wasn't on parole in Oakland.

After thanking Edna and promising again to come to the party, I rang off and phoned John Scopes. He wasn't in, but I talked to Sarah, who told me no body had turned up yet. They'd call if one did.

Aldo put me on hold for about ten minutes when I phoned back. He was probably getting even for being railroaded, and I guess I deserved it. He was doing me a favor. I should be grateful. But sometimes a girl could endure so much. While I waited, I dreamed of a cold beer. More than anything I was thirsty. Finally Aldo came back on the line.

"Sorry," he said. "I didn't mean for you to wait so long. My boss came by."

"That's okay. No problem," I said, and figured we were even. Somewhere, in the back of my mind, a voice was saying, *This is not a healthy relationship.*

"Let's see. Wilson, Lon. Here it is. Lots of felony priors. Heavy dude. Three-time loser. Assault with a deadly weapon, assault with intent, and a manslaughter charge. Convictions. Time. Good behavior, early release, then back in for carrying on parole." He snorted into the phone. "Listen to this one. He took a pistol to his parole meeting. Looks like your man's a real brain-o."

"Is he in or out now?"

"Out. Last known address—you want it?"

"Please."

"Thirteen twenty-five Thirty-second Avenue. In the city."

I jotted that down. "What about a phone?"

He gave it to me, and I hung up before he could ask why I wanted to know all of this. He should have asked first, but most of the time he forgot.

I used my last two dimes to phone Wilson, but after fifteen rings I gave up, fished my dimes out of the slot, and headed back over the bridge.

12

Thirteen twenty-five Thirty-second Avenue was in a gray part of town called the Sunset: lower-middle-class, not much green, and a lot of drab stucco. It wasn't close enough to the ocean to be scenic, just near enough to get the perpetual fog on a daily basis.

There weren't any black BMWs in sight, so I parked, stayed in my car, and checked out the house from across the street. No burglar alarm, but that was okay, I wasn't planning to break in. The place was a narrow two-story structure, shabbier than the others on the block. A house instead of a home like its neighbors. Curtains were pulled across two picture windows on the first floor, and the little patch of grass in front was yellowed and trampled. The paint, a faded coral, was chipped and weathered, just like the stucco it was supposed to cover. An attached garage was closed, padlocked, and windowless. If I had to bet on it, I'd bet nobody was home.

I pushed open the car door and strolled casually up the walk. Up close the place definitely looked abandoned. I tapped on the door and waited. Nothing.

The door had one of those peephole viewers you can look through to see who's there, but that was the sum-total effort at security. The lock was a spring-bolt type, a cinch to manipulate, but in quiet neighborhoods like these, there were usually a thousand eyes behind the drawn curtains. Besides, without an alarm system, where was the fun? I knocked again, then tried the doorknob, but it held fast.

I backed away a couple of steps and looked around. The house was wedged in between two others so that it shared a common wall on either side. If I wanted to get to the backyard to see what I could see, I'd have to go through a neighbor's house to do it. Not likely, but I'd talk to them anyway.

I glanced at the house on my right. Its owner would probably be more receptive than the one on the left with all the bars across its windows.

A solid minute after I rang the bell the door cracked open the length of its safety chain, and weepy gray eyes the color of the fog stared out at me. From the inch or two of exposed face I couldn't tell if I was looking at a man or a woman. All I could make out was that the person behind the door was very old and very scared.

"Yes?" Still no clue as to gender.

I smiled, and introduced myself as a private investigator. "I'm looking for your next-door neighbor, Lon Wilson. He's not home, so I thought I could catch him at work. Do you know where he works?"

"In some kind of trouble, is he?"

"Not really. I just need to see him."

He—or she—thought it over. "Never talked to the boy myself. Don't know that he works at all." This time the voice sounded decidedly feminine.

"Oh." I smiled again. The opening in the doorway

wasn't any wider, but it hadn't closed yet either. "I didn't catch your name," I said.

"That's because I didn't give it. It's Mrs. Topolski, and if you ask me, he's out of town." The watery eyes sharpened. "He hasn't been home in two days."

"What makes you think that?"

"The newspaper."

I glanced over at Wilson's empty yard. "What newspaper?"

"He usually takes the evening paper, but it didn't come tonight. Didn't come yesterday. I figure he's out of town. In fact I don't *think* it, I *know* it. I sleep light, and that boy keeps all hours. Sometimes he'll come home at midnight and I'll hear him come in. Sometimes it's three in the morning, sometimes five. I hear him all the time and, come to think of it, I haven't heard a thing lately." She paused to wet her lips and grabbed on to the doorjamb for support. "It's that front door of his. I wish Ezra'd fix it. That's what happens when you rent a place out, you just don't keep it up. Ezra was good when he lived here. When he moved to Minnesota, he promised he'd keep the place up—property values and all—but just look at it now. It's in his interest, don't you think?"

"Absolutely."

"Now look at it. Pish," she said in disgust.

I glanced across the yard to Wilson's front door.

"You pretty much can see who comes and goes next door, can't you, Mrs. Topolski?"

"If I happen to be near the window, I notice who's there." What little I could see of the old lady's face looked positively coy.

"Have you ever seen a big man come by, black hair, white streak at the temple? Has anyone like that been to see Lon lately?"

"No."

I wanted her to think longer, to search her memory, but the old lady was positive. A thought suddenly occurred to me. "What's Lon Wilson look like? Is he skinny and dark-haired? Does he ever wear a blue windbreaker?"

"Never. He's tall and muscle-bound. Got a crop of curly orange hair you just can't mistake." She stared hard at me. "You sure he's the one you want?"

So much for that hunch. I produced my business card and fed it through the crack in the door. "Will you call me if he comes home?"

"What if it's three in the morning?"

"That's fine. I want to know."

Mrs. Topolski took the card and clutched the door. Her damp eyes gleamed with a new excitement. I glanced over at Wilson's yard again. "Newspapers, huh? You make a pretty good detective, Mrs. Topolski. Ever thought about getting into the business?"

"Pish," the old lady said, but she smiled before she closed the door.

Nobody answered at the house with the bars on it, or at any of the other ones I tried across the street. I checked my watch when I got into the Citroën. It was close to seven. Pretty much a strikeout of a day. Best thing to do was head home and reassess.

Just as I reached the end of the street, I checked the rearview mirror out of habit. What I saw made me sit up and pay attention: A black BMW had just rounded the corner at the opposite end of the street.

I circled the block and parked five doors down from Wilson's house, half a block down from Pete August's gleaming car. Slouched in my seat, I watched him amble up the walk and knock at the front door. He waited a couple of minutes, tried the doorknob, then tried the neighbors. He was doing everything I'd done with one exception: He hadn't checked to see if anyone was watching.

Mrs. Topolski didn't answer when he rang her doorbell. Too bad. She probably could have found out why he wanted Wilson.

August finally gave up and sauntered back to his car. When he drove away, I fell in behind him and passed Mrs. Topolski's house. The old lady waved at me from her doorway and pointed down the road to where August had disappeared. I laughed out loud, waved back at her, and raced after August.

13

As it turned out, I would have been better off staking out Wilson's place. August didn't go anywhere more exciting than his office. I hung around outside, ducking whenever a night cruiser passed, and alternating between boredom and jealousy. August had to have loads of paying cases to keep him at the office so late.

By eleven o'clock I remembered I was hungry. The avocado omelet and Bloody Mary from lunch seemed like a decade ago. I held out for another half hour, then headed home, stopping by an all-night pizza place that sold by the slice. I bought two slices and ate them while I traded jokes with the guy behind the counter, then went home and prayed for sleep.

Most nights I never slept at all. That's why I started running. Exhaustion helps sometimes. But most nights were like this one, when all I could do was lie awake for hours, bathed in yellow neon from the bar sign outside my window, wondering what might have been if I were different, if I'd wanted a family, a home life, like Mitch wanted.

It didn't seem to matter that we'd both turned into vengeful monsters the minute we said our vows—something about feeling tied down made me crazy and mean. At least that was my take on it. What Mitch's problem was I'd yet to figure out.

We knew early on it wasn't working, and when it was finally over, we were both relieved. The part that I couldn't understand was why, eight years later, I was still losing sleep over what I knew in my head would never have worked for either of us.

The next morning the phone woke me, but I was too groggy to pick it up before the machine did. My recorded voice lilted irritatingly over the line while I fumbled for the receiver and switched the tape off.

"Hello?"

"Is this Tuxedo Messages?" a bewildered female voice asked. "Myra's Tuxedo Messages?"

"What? No—right, yes it is," I said, sitting up and running a hand through my tangled hair while I silently cursed my cousin. "Uh, yeah. Any message you want by tuxedoed messenger."

"Good. That's exactly what I want."

I scrabbled for a pen and paper and took down the information. "We charge extra for Marin or East Bay. The bridges, you know. Tolls, mileage."

"That's fine. I just want him to listen to what I have to say. This should get his attention."

"Right." I hung up and groaned when I looked at the clock. Eleven.

Late mornings were becoming a habit. I knew I should be worrying about scaring up my next case, my next *paying* case, but I had rent money for the next three months, so where was the rush? Finding August's motive for the murder wasn't going to take any three months, I was sure of that. There'd be plenty of time later.

I stretched, slipped into a pair of running shorts and a T-shirt, and hit the street.

The run went well: no murders, no policemen, no black-and-white-haired murderers. Nothing but tranquil, brainwashing rhythm. I considered running by the Coast Guard house to see Sarah Scopes but decided against it, mostly because I just didn't want to think about the case anymore and partly because, for once, Mitch's advice—to steer clear of the scene of the crime—didn't seem so crazy. If Pete August or anybody else wanted to hurt me, I didn't want to make it easy for them by being too predictable. Besides, Golden Gate Park was a nice place to run.

When I got to Harry's party, it was good to see the old man again. He'd been kind to me, understanding when I told him I needed out of the bureaucracy. He even threw a couple of cases my way after I got set up.

I had chips and bean dip for breakfast and listened to the agency head read a short farewell speech that sounded too much like a eulogy. Afterward, halfway through a slice of *brazo gitano* that Cecil Flores's wife had made, I heard someone behind me mention Robert Purdue. When I turned around, I found Leon Moore and Sally Connors, two hardworking but uninspired probation officers.

"Did you say Purdue? Gummy Purdue?" I asked.

"That's right," Leon said. "Did you know him?"

"*Did?* What happened to him?"

Sally stepped between me and Leon. "He passed away, Ronnie." Her voice was low and confidential.

"He's dead? When? How?"

Sally started to answer, but Leon beat her to it.

"Landlord found him. You know, his emphysema. I'm surprised the dude lasted as long as he did."

"Isn't it just terrible? I know he was trying to stay straight," Sally added, flashing Leon a dirty look.

"When did it happen?"

"They found him this morning," Leon said just as Edna came up behind him.

"Are you talking about poor old Gummy Purdue?" she asked.

"Yeah," Leon answered. "Did you know Ronnie knew him?"

"No kidding?" Edna gave me a strange look. "I thought he was after your time."

"He was," I said. "I met him through somebody else." Each of the three faces around me registered different degrees of curiosity. "Whose case was he?"

"Mine," Edna said, and I changed the subject. But the first chance I got, I steered her away from Leon and Sally and into a corner.

"Can we talk about Purdue a minute?" I asked.

"There isn't much to say."

"That's all right. Your office still where it used to be?"

Edna led me down the hall into a narrow, windowless cube. She was smaller than me and Asian, with a wide oval face, a ready smile, and perfect posture.

Ballet posters covered one wall of her office, and plants overflowed the desk and a bookshelf. A little plaque on the wall said, Visualize World Peace. Edna glided into one of two chairs in front of the desk and turned guileless almond-shaped eyes on me.

"What's up?" she asked.

Those eyes were Edna's secret weapon. None of her cases—except maybe Robert Purdue—would ever betray the open trust in those eyes. I never did figure it out, but the cons never, ever tried to con Edna.

"Will they do an autopsy?"

"Should they?"

"I don't know. What're they giving as his cause of death?"

"Asphyxiation. His air tank was empty. From all appearances he'd been drinking and forgot to pick up a fresh one." She paused, studying me. "You don't think it was an accident?"

"He's tied in with a case I'm working. I talked to him about a man I saw commit murder. The city cops don't seem to want to be bothered to look into it so . . ."

"You're helping them out, and they don't know you are," she finished.

I thought of the black-and-white that had followed me from the Hall of Justice to August's office. "Not exactly," I said. "I think they do know."

"Ronnie, Ronnie." Edna was shaking her head. "I thought you said you're not supposed to work on things the police are working on. Can't you get into trouble that way?"

I started to deny it, but smiled instead. Edna wouldn't believe me anyway. "I guess I could. But it's not really an open case. If it were, somebody would be putting some effort into it. Right now they're just looking the other way, trying to cover it up or pretend it never happened."

"But why?"

I met my friend's level gaze. "That's just it, I don't know. The guy who did it is so well thought of that nobody believes me. It's not likely the body'll turn up, since the killer threw it into the Bay. It's probably halfway to China by now. On top of everything the lieutenant in charge hates me."

"Is it OPD?"

"No. It's Philly Post."

"Uh-oh. I've heard about him. He eats scorpions for breakfast," Edna said, and I had to laugh. "Too bad it didn't happen in Oakland, I know a couple of cops who might help you out. What can I do besides push an autopsy? Want me to talk to your detective, put in a good word for you from the Oakland Parole Office?"

"Thanks, Edna, but maybe you'd better not." I couldn't ask her to get involved. There was nothing except Pete August tying the two incidents together, and as far as Post was concerned, August walked on water. No, I'd have to tell Post about Purdue's connection myself.

"Just keep what I've told you in mind. That's all I can ask for now."

Edna nodded and smiled. "I think I can handle that. Now." She opened the door. "Let's see if they left us any *lumpia*."

14

"A snitch is a snitch," Philly Post told me.

He'd stood up the moment I walked into his office and refused to sit back down. Instead he listened from behind his desk, leaning forward with both fists centered on two even stacks of paper while I stood, too, and told him about August and Purdue. While I talked, I tried not to notice the way his frown deepened with every word.

"Talking to somebody doesn't mean you killed him," he said when I finished. "You talked to Purdue yourself. Are you a suspect?"

"I'm here, aren't I? Has August come forward?"

"Not yet."

"And you're not asking him to either." Post said nothing and I tried to unclench my teeth. He was starting to get on my nerves. "So you're not going to lose any sleep over this, is that it?"

He dropped into his chair and rubbed his eyes with a thumb and forefinger, then ran his hand across his forehead and crumpled up his bushy eyebrows.

"Purdue had so many people on his ass," he said. "I

can think of fifteen just off the top of my head that would
want him out. But I'm not hauling them all in for questioning just because the man forgot to get a refill on his
air tank."

"Are you at least going to talk to August? Ask him
about Purdue and Wilson?"

He let his hand drop onto the desk with an impatient
thud. "Is that what you think I ought to do? Is that it? I
missed it entirely, didn't I? You want me to pull in the
only guy in town *without* a motive." He leaned back in
his chair and shook his head. "That would clinch my
promotion. No body, no motive, *but I've got my man.*"
He waved to dismiss me. "Ventana, you're wasting my
time and yours."

"Not to mention the cop's who you've assigned to harass me."

His eyes disappeared under his eyebrows when he sat
up and frowned. Suddenly he was paying attention again.
"What are you talking about?"

"Get straight with me, Post. Don't deny you're trying
to intimidate me with one of your uniforms."

"Don't bluff me, Ventana."

"I'm not."

"You got a name? A badge number?"

If he was acting, he was damn good at it. And if he
wasn't, who sicced Officer Ryan on me?

"Give me a name," he said.

"Never mind." I stood up. "But if you are looking for
a promotion, Lieutenant Post, I think you should at least
question August. Find out where he was last night.
There's something wrong here, and if you don't catch it,
somebody else will."

He held me with his impassive face, eyes deep set under his eyebrows.

"This case is open, Ventana. I haven't assigned anyone to harass you, that's not how I work. But if I catch you within a mile of any of the principals, you're dead. I'll—"

"Yank my license before I know what hit me?" I let my hand rest on the doorknob a second longer than I really needed to. "I'm sure you will. As usual, Lieutenant, it's been nice talking to you."

I sauntered out feeling peevish and annoyed. Post was so busy telling himself August had nothing to do with it that he was letting the whole mess slip right by him. And I wasn't exactly getting through to him either.

On my way to a pay phone downstairs I ran into Martha Coyle.

"You're Blackie's friend, aren't you?" she said when she stopped me in the corridor. Somehow the judge managed to look friendly without smiling. "Are you testifying in a case today?"

"Not exactly. Just visiting the cops."

"I see. Is it the same problem of the other night or something new?"

"A little bit of both," I said, surprised she remembered. We stood there a couple of seconds, looking each other over without saying anything. There was a kind of weird tension in the air, and it wasn't coming from me. Before I started to feel too uncomfortable, she smiled.

"I hope the lieutenant was more cooperative today."

How much had Blackie told her? "Right," I said. "In a couple of years I figure we'll be sending each other Christmas cards."

"I take it things didn't go well?"

I shrugged, and she glanced at her watch. "I'd better go. It was nice to see you again, Ms. Ventana. Give my regards to Mr. Coogan."

I watched her disappear into an elevator and wondered

what it was about her that made me think she was un-
happy. I liked her, and she came across well. She was a
looker, like Blackie said, and very successful. But something, maybe the tension she gave out and couldn't hide
just by looking calm, messed things up. I couldn't really
put a finger on what it was, so I just shrugged, fished for
coins in my wallet, and headed for the phones to check
the answering machine for messages. There was only one.

"Hello? Hello? Miss Ventana? Are you there? This is
Mrs. Topolski on Thirty-second Avenue. He's here." She
hung up.

I checked my watch. It was four o'clock. Mrs. Topolski hadn't said what time she called. I looked up her
number, slipped another couple of dimes into the slot,
and dialed. It rang five times before she answered.

"Mrs. Topolski, this is Ronnie Ventana. I just got your
message. Is he still there?"

"No. But I think he's coming back tonight."

"Oh?"

"Yes. The newspaper has been delivered since he left."

"Good work," I said. "You're a great detective. I don't
think I'll be home tonight, but I'll keep checking my
messages until I hear from you again, okay? Thanks."

I called John Scopes, got Sarah, again. Still no floater.
I was beginning to doubt he'd ever surface. Probably, like
I told Edna, he was halfway to China.

A black-and-white followed me out of the parking lot
across from the Hall of Justice. Except for the fact that
they'd made the Citroën, I didn't care; I was just going
home. But I stopped even for yellow lights and signaled
before I made any turns. I waved at Officer Ryan when I
pulled up in front of the apartment, but he just drove by
and pretended he didn't see me. If Post didn't know anything about him, then why did Ryan end up following me

every time I talked to Post? The man deserved an Oscar. And I deserved a drink.

When I stopped off at the Quarter Moon Saloon for a beer, naturally Blackie was there. He offered to buy the first round if I bought the second, so we had a couple and I told him about being tailed, about Purdue, and about Post's reaction.

"What'd you expect, doll?" he asked when I finished.

"Blackie, I know somebody dumped Purdue. The way he nursed that tank, I can't imagine he'd forget to get a refill."

"Forget it. You can't touch it now, babe. The P.D.'s into it. Leave it alone." He slid his chair back and grinned. "Come on," he said. "I'm starved. Let's get something down the street."

"I'm not hungry."

"You can watch. I need the company."

"Sure, right." I checked my phone machine upstairs to see if Mrs. Topolski had called, then walked two doors down with Blackie to a burger joint where the waitress knew us both by name. Once I smelled the patties sizzling on the grill, I changed my mind and ordered.

"I can't leave it alone," I said when Alma set two steaming bacon burgers in front of us. I picked up a french fry and nibbled at it. "Nobody's doing anything about it. The military police need remedial lessons in thinking, and Philly Post is just sitting on it. It's like *I'm* the criminal for bringing it up."

Blackie reached into his pocket and popped the cap off the beer he'd brought over from the Quarter Moon. "You never went up against August before." He took a long swig from the bottle. "The guy is slick, didn't I tell you? If you know what's good for you, you'll keep away from him *and* the cops. They're not going to help you, Ventana, not even your little friend, Aldo."

"But—"

"Those guys stick together like slime on a slug. Leave it alone. You don't owe the dead guy nothing. You don't even know who he is or why old Petey offed him." He picked up his hamburger and pointed it at me. "If they didn't know what you know, it'd be different. But they're watching you now. You said so yourself."

I sighed and chewed my hamburger without tasting it. Blackie ate, too, but with gusto, like he hadn't eaten in a week. He washed it all down with beer, then looked at me, and his handsome, grizzled face softened.

"You want to get at the truth, don't you?"

I shrugged.

"Kid, the world just ain't like that." He pointed at the hamburger I hadn't finished. "You done with that?"

"Sure, go ahead." I shoved my plate across the table to him. He ate it, then said, "Let's get out of here, doll."

I turned down his invitation to hear a new sax player jam in a club down in Hayward because I wanted to stay local in case Mrs. Topolski called. When I went upstairs to check the machine, the little red light was blinking like a firefly in the dark. I played the single message back, laughed out loud at the excitement in Mrs. Topolski's voice, and headed for the Sunset.

Halfway there I was seized with the sudden sensation that I was being followed. The rearview mirror didn't show anybody special, but I doubled back just to be safe, then circled around and did all the things you're supposed to do to shake a tail. I even parked in a driveway for a while, but nobody in the cars that passed showed any interest. I felt like a fool, silly and paranoid.

Nobody followed me the rest of the way, and when I

pulled up outside Wilson's house, my stomach gave a little flip. The curtains were still drawn, but slivers of light edged the window. A dark ten-year-old Camaro sat in the drive.

I gave myself a little pep talk as I walked up the sidewalk, then took a deep breath and knocked. The big red-haired man who opened the door turned on the porch light almost as an afterthought. I guessed he was in his early twenties, a pumping-iron kind of guy, with tattoos and muscles straining the sleeves of his Rambo T-shirt. He had a flat, freckled face and a head that looked pea-sized next to his neck, shoulders, and chest. He grinned at me, mildly curious. His eyes were astonishingly green, long-lashed, like a woman's.

"Yeah?" He cracked his knuckles—loud, bone-crunching popping noises that almost made me lose my nerve. "You selling something, or did my dream just come true?"

Romeo he was not. "Neither," I said. "Are you Lon Wilson?"

"Yeah?" He eyed me up and down, the grin never leaving his face.

"My name's Veronica Ventana. I'm a private investigator. Can I talk to you for a minute?"

The careless grin faltered. "I've got nothing to say to no investigator." He started to close the door.

"Wait!" I caught a flash of movement next door: Mrs. Topolski. What a backup. "Please," I said. "I have information you need to hear."

He blocked the entrance with his pumped-up torso. "What?"

"Can I come inside?" I wasn't sure I wanted to, but a person could learn a lot just seeing where, and how, somebody lives. If he said no, I wouldn't push it, but

Wilson just shrugged and stepped back to let me in. Somebody his size didn't need to be afraid of anybody.

Three paces put me into the center of a small room that looked even smaller with him in it. He dwarfed the plaid couch and chairs; the only piece of furniture that looked sturdy enough to hold him was the simulated leather lounger in front of the television. The screen flickered. The two naked women on the screen wore military caps and nothing else. They were doing strange things to a naked man. I watched them spray what looked like shaving cream all over each other. When they started licking the stuff off, I figured it had to be whipped cream.

"What information?" Wilson asked, folding his arms across his massive chest.

I glanced up at him, then back at the screen. "What is this? I've never seen anything like it."

He grunted, leaned over, and turned it off. I think he was blushing. "What information?"

"Mind if I sit down?" If I was going to be bold, I might as well do it right. I took one of the plaid chairs, and he swiveled the lounger to face me, then dropped into it. The chair let out a little sigh when his body settled into it. He picked up a can of beer from the table next to the chair, shook it, then set it back down.

"What do you want?" he said.

"Go ahead," I told him, nodding at the empty beer can. "I won't steal anything. And, no thanks, I don't care for one myself."

He went into the kitchen and reappeared a second later with a refill in his hand.

"What's this hot information?" he said.

"Have you ever heard of Pete August?"

He blinked. "Should I?"

"He's a private investigator. He used to work for the D.A.'s office."

"So? What's that got to do with me?"

"He's looking for you." No reaction. "Do you have any idea why?"

"Is that the hot news?"

"I was hoping you could tell me why he's so interested in you."

"The only guy I help around here is old Lon Wilson. I done my time. I'm not looking to do more." He settled back into the lounger, holding the can in his meaty fist.

"What about Gummy Purdue?"

"What about him?"

"August asked him to find you. The next day Purdue turned up dead."

The square, freckled face closed up. "I don't guess I know anything about it," he said.

"You're not in a very good spot, Mr. Wilson."

He pushed himself out of the chair and filled the room up again. "Oh, yeah? So how come the cops haven't been by?"

"They haven't made the right connections yet."

"There ain't none."

"There's me."

"What is that—a threat?"

"No, it's a fact. I don't like to talk to the police if I can avoid it."

He rubbed the back of his neck and looked me up and down again. "Don't drag me into it," he finally said.

"Convince me not to."

He hesitated, eyeing me. Then he set the can down. "Gummy told him I knew where to find Jake Murieta. That's all he wanted with me. I told him I didn't know, and that was the end of it."

"So you have talked to August. When?"

"Last week."

"Didn't he talk to you a couple of days ago? Yesterday?"

"I seen him once, last week. I been outta town since then."

"What did he want with Jake Murieta?"

"If you want answers, talk to Jake. I don't know where he is, but like I told August, ask around the Mission. Jake'll turn up."

"What's he look like?"

"He's a spic," Wilson said, like that was all I needed to know. He reached over and turned on the television set. There were four men on the screen now.

I reached into my pocket for a business card. "If August gets in touch with you again, will you call me?"

Wilson kept his eyes on the tangle of arms and legs on the screen. "Hey, I'm outta this thing."

I tossed the card on top of the television set anyway. "In case you change your mind," I said, then stepped around him and slipped out the door. Mrs. Topolski's silhouette waved from the window next door as I drove away.

15

"**C**ome on, Rogelio. Be a sport."

The short, olive-skinned man working over the blackened industrial stove acted like he hadn't even heard me. He had the suave, dark good looks of most well-bred Latin men and seemed out of place in the cluttered restaurant kitchen. It was about thirty degrees hotter here than it was in the next room, where the tables were all filled up and there was a line at the door.

"Veronica," he said, and smiled through his thick Pancho Villa mustache. He rolled his *r*'s like a caress. "Can't you see I'm just a lowly restaurant cook?"

"Owner."

He shrugged humbly. "I only make tacos, burritos, refried beans. I know nothing of gangsters or hit men."

I grinned. "I know, I know. You walk the straight and narrow. Rogelio, I've heard it all before."

"One lives longer that way, *mi hija.*" He stuffed a handful of tortillas into a stainless-steel box and pushed a button. The box hissed, and steam feathered out from the uneven seal around its door. "Your words," he said, and jabbed the button again.

"I'm not with the parole office anymore, Rogelio. You don't have to convince me. Besides, I know you're not going to get involved with any jerks like you did before. You were just a kid then."

He nodded, and waited for the steam to clear, then reached inside the box with a set of tongs. Four tortillas went into one basket and six into another. He shoved two plates loaded with corn-husk tamales, rice, and beans onto the counter next to the stove. *"Tía! Tía!"*

A gaunt middle-aged woman, Rogelio's aunt, took the plates from the other side.

"Andale, pues," Rogelio called after her, with a wink at me. "See how happy we are? My aunt, my mother, my sister, and me. We do not speak to this thug, Murieta. Whatever you want to know about him is bad. Don't look for trouble, Veronica."

"If I had a choice, I wouldn't. Is he pretty heavy-duty?"

Rogelio set a plate in front of me. "This," he said, ignoring my question, "is heavy-duty: my new recipe for chile relleno. You will like it."

I glanced at the crisp, golden mound in front of me. "It looks terrific," I said, "but I ate already. Come on, Rogelio, I need to know. Does he have any ties with the *Nuestra Familia*?"

Rogelio put a fork in my hand. "Taste it," he commanded.

I sighed, took a bite, and savored it. Cheese and batter and pepper melted in my mouth. "It's fantastic," I said. "Delicious." I took another bite, then another, and didn't set my fork down until it was gone.

"That was great." I dabbed at my mouth with a paper napkin. "Now, what about Murieta?"

Rogelio picked up my empty plate and stacked it with others on the counter. "He is dangerous," he said, his back to me.

"Is he involved?"

Rogelio turned and cocked an eyebrow, but said nothing.

"Is he in the *Nuestra Familia*?"

"He is not that dangerous," Rogelio said.

"What's the big deal, then? If he's not Mexican Mafia . . . I just want to know where the man lives, that's all."

He came back to the counter, an easy, teasing grin on his face. "Veronica, you should marry again. Have some babies this time. Forget all this *mierda*."

I laughed. "When *you* ask me, I will. Say the word, and I'm yours."

He was grinning. "Quit first, then we will talk."

"No way. A girl's got to make a living."

"*Dí le*, Rogelio. Tell her."

We both looked up. His aunt smiled at both of us from the kitchen door, then turned her mournful black eyes on Rogelio.

"Tell her, *mi hijo*. She wouldn't ask if she didn't need to know. We owe so much."

Rogelio sighed, pulled some taco shells out of the frying vat, and glanced over his shoulder at his aunt. She urged him on with a nod, then left us alone, taking a tray overflowing with plates out the door. The rush of cool air from the dining room stirred the savory aromas in the kitchen: chiles and beef, onion and garlic, and the hot corn scent of the tortillas.

"Jake Murieta has a green-and-yellow house," Rogelio

said softly, avoiding my eyes, "on the corner of Twenty-fifth and Utah, next door to the playground."

"What does he look like?"

"Dark, slender, a mustache. About my height. Doesn't dress like he's got lots of money, but he drives a real nice car, a white Lincoln."

I smiled. "Sounds dangerous to me."

Rogelio didn't smile back. *"Cuidado, mi hija,"* he said. "Be careful."

I found the house without any problem, even in the dark. It was late, too late to go knocking on any doors, but I did anyway. Nobody answered, so I just sat outside awhile, watching. It was too dark to tell if the place was wired. There weren't any decals on the windows, and no digital pad outside the door, which were the usual clues, but somehow this didn't feel like the right kind of neighborhood to go exploring. After about an hour I gave up, started the engine, and drove home.

There were five messages on my phone machine. Three were Tuxedo Message requests—I'd have to call them back in the morning. One was from Aldo, and one from a drunk-on-his-ass Blackie. His message was he was having fun and didn't I want to have fun too?

"Remember the redhead from AIA? Well, I found her and we're down the street at Bimbo's. Why don't you—?" Beep. The machine cut him off, but it was just as well.

"Sorry, Blackie," I said out loud, and pulled my last beer out of the fridge. Then I curled up on the couch to watch David Letterman close out the night.

16

The run went well the next morning, a little over five miles down along the Embarcadero and back, cleansing and soothing. After a shower and scrambled eggs on the hot plate, I sat down at the table by the phone, the one I called my desk. I had one Tuxedo Message for today at one o'clock. When I returned the three calls from yesterday, I had two more for that afternoon and one for next week. And Myra had said May was a slow month. I phoned Aldo.

"I overheard something you could be interested in," he said.

"About who?"

"I'd rather not say over the phone. Are you free for lunch?"

What did he get out of these lunches anyway? I sighed. "Give me a hint, Aldo. Is it worth my while?"

"Isn't it always?"

"That's debatable. What's this about?"

"Your friend."

"August?"

"Right."

He'd said he wasn't going to help me anymore, but something had obviously changed his mind, probably the fact that I'd backed off. The last time he'd pulled his tight little ethics on me and cut me off, I'd kept after him until he quit talking to me. Finally *I'd* had to invite *him* to lunch.

"Why can't you just tell me over the phone?"

"I'd rather not."

"All right, Aldo. Lunch. But it's got to be an early one. I've got to be someplace at one." Aldo hated early lunches.

"How about tomorrow?"

"Tomorrow's worse," I lied. If he had something on August, I wanted to know now.

"And the next day?"

"If I have to wait that long, I won't care what you've got."

"Oh, all right." He sighed loudly over the line. I got the point: Aldo wasn't happy. "How about Bennie's Café? Eleven?"

"Eleven thirty."

Another sigh. "Okay. See you there."

I had just enough time to drive over to the Mission district before meeting Aldo. In daylight the house looked like it belonged to the playground next door. The yellow-and-green paint job on the exterior matched the multicolored slides and swings and the merry-go-round. I pulled up in front and got out. If Murieta was as dangerous as Rogelio made him out to be, I wanted to be as conspicuous about seeing him as possible.

The door had a bronze crucifix centered over its glossy yellow facade. When I rang the bell, a little girl of about eight opened it, then called out for her mother and hung around to watch. Somebody shouted something in Spanish from the back of the house, then a stout woman of about fifty loomed out of the shadows of the tunnellike hall inside.

Her face was as plump as the rest of her, with high cheekbones and skin that glistened like copper. Dark, curious eyes met mine.

"Yes?"

"Are you Mrs. Murieta?"

"Yes?"

"Is Mr. Murieta home? Jake Murieta?"

The friendly openness drained from her face. "*Jacobo?* No, he is not home. I am sorry," she said, and stood there looking like she'd like to close the door in my face but was too polite to do it.

"Is he at work? Maybe I could catch him there?"

"No. My husband, he—he is away."

"Out of town?" Something flickered in the darkness behind the woman. Past her shoulder, in the dusky hall, enormous brown eyes, innocent and scared, stared back at me. They were the eyes of a young woman, a girl's eyes.

Mrs. Murieta followed my gaze, hissed something in Spanish, and the girl shrank away, back into the darkness. When Mrs. Murieta turned back to me, she frowned.

"I am so sorry. *Jacobo* won't be back for a while."

"Maybe you can help, then. I'm not really looking for Mr. Murieta. I just want to know if somebody's talked to him. The man I'm looking for is about six feet tall, heavy, with black hair and a shock of white at the temple. His name's Pete August. Has anybody like that been by to see him in the last couple of days?"

The woman shook her head.

"If he does come by, will you call me?"

"Of course, *señorita*. I will call immediately." Mrs. Murieta started to close the door.

"Wait a sec! Here's my card. It's got my number on it. Will you ask Mr. Murieta to phone me when you speak to him?"

"Yes, yes, of course." As the door swung shut, I caught one last glimpse of the dark, innocent eyes staring at me from the gloom inside.

17

A generous person would have described Bennie's Café as a diner, but a realistic one would have called it a dive. It was close to the Hall of Justice, which wasn't in such a hot neighborhood to begin with, but not many cops went there, mostly because Bennie's competitor across the street had a flashier sign and served beer for a nickel less. On the positive side Bennie's grill was cleaner, and so were his counters. The food wasn't that great, but the privacy was. In fact when I walked in and found Aldo there waiting, it was just me, Aldo, and Bennie.

"Nice tux, Ronnie," Bennie said.

"Thanks. I'll take a grilled cheese, Bennie. Fries and a beer," I said as I passed him on my way to Aldo's booth in the back. Bennie was already working a hamburger on the grill, probably destined for Aldo.

Aldo, in all his neatly pressed officialdom, didn't look delighted to see me. He didn't even comment on Myra's tux. Hardly the reception I'd expected. I smiled at him when I sat down, but he didn't smile back.

"Uh-oh. Am I in trouble?"

"Dammit, Ronnie! You lied to me." His face looked comically fierce, uncannily like an angry Kermit the Frog.

"About what?"

"You told me Wilson wasn't part of the August thing."

I acted surprised. "You mean he is?"

"Of course he is. I rode down the elevator with Lieutenant Post today. He was talking to somebody else and you know who he mentioned? Lon Wilson!" Aldo looked like he wanted to cry. "And now I've stuck my nose in the whole thing. I could get suspended. Or fired."

"Relax, Aldo. Cops don't get canned for stuff like that. You've got to do something major, like take a bribe, and even then they've got to prove it."

"But Lieutenant Post—"

"You didn't tell him, did you?"

"I should have."

I relaxed. Post didn't know. "Look, Aldo. I never said it wasn't related to August. You just assumed it wasn't. I didn't lie to you, Aldo. I'd never lie about something like that."

Bennie brought over the hamburger and the grilled cheese. He looked as greasy as the food on the plates. "I'm with Aldo," he said. "A cop's got to keep up with his integrity, you know."

I glared at Bennie and he shrank back behind the counter. Aldo took a big, consoling mouthful of his hamburger.

"Lighten up, Aldo. Nobody knows about Wilson. Besides, all you gave me was his address. Big deal. You're not going to lose your job over that." He took another bite and refused to look at me. "Listen to me, Aldo. I'm sorry. Okay? You're not going to get canned. I promise."

Bennie showed up again, this time with my beer.

"She's right about that." Aldo looked up, and the cook nodded sagely. That, and another bite from his hamburger, seemed to satisfy Aldo.

"So what did Post say about Wilson?" I asked while he was chewing and his expression was halfway back to normal.

Aldo had probably been taught to chew each mouthful one hundred times. He swallowed, then said, "Mostly it had to do with you trying to tell him how to do his job. He really doesn't like you, Ronnie."

"No kidding? Is he going to talk to Wilson?"

"He didn't say."

I picked up my sandwich, then set it down again. "What were you going to tell me about August?"

Aldo hesitated. "In light of what's happened, I don't think you need to know."

"Oh, come on, Aldo. Do you want me to beg?" He didn't answer. "Okay," I said, rising, "I've got to go."

"But your lunch."

I edged out of the booth. "You eat it, Aldo. I can't stay."

I slipped a bill on the table. "It's on me."

18

The guy I delivered the message to in Mill Valley was an architect; the message was from his ex-girlfriend. She wanted him back even though he'd left her and moved in with his analyst. His answer was no.

The other two messages, one for two thirty and the other for three, were in the city, so I drove back across the bridge and stopped by to see Officer Tucker on the way.

His office was in a beautifully maintained mission adobe painted beige with a red tile roof. Inside, though, the early California effect was lost. It was strictly government issue: metal desks and chairs, all painted olive drab or gunmetal gray. When Tucker saw me in Myra's tuxedo, he grinned.

"Don't you look cute? You didn't have to dress up just for me."

He laughed just like I pictured a quarter-pounder would. I forced a smile. "I didn't. It's for my job."

"I thought you said you were a private investigator."

"I am. How's your investigation going?"

"Oh, you mean the alleged murder?" Tucker must have been talking to Post. He shook his head and shuffled through some folders on his desk. "Nope. No body yet. Case is still open, though."

"John Scopes hasn't given up, has he?"

"He's not dragging the Bay, if that's what you mean, but he's keeping his eyes open. The city cops think you're full of feathers, you know that?"

"I sort of got that impression. What about you?"

He tipped his chair back and propped a leg up on his desk. "Me? I don't know." He squinted at me. "I haven't given it much thought."

Not too surprising. He probably needed all his mental powers just to button his shirt in the morning.

"My boss and I were doing a little research on this thing. Could be, we don't even have jurisdiction. Could be, it's the FBI's. Federal property and whatnot."

"What does that mean? Would they investigate instead of the city?"

"Could be. That's why we're looking into it. I'll tell you what. Just go on like you are for now and keep working with the city police and us. If we find out any different, I'll let you know. Personally. How does that sound?"

"Call me the minute you find anything out." I checked my watch and stood. "I've got to go," I said. "But if anything turns up—anything at all—let me know."

"Will do."

The prospect of ditching Philly Post made my mouth water.

The last two Tuxedo Messages went quickly, and by three thirty I was back home. Somebody had called twice but hadn't left a message. That wasn't unusual. A lot of people hate answering machines and I can't blame them. I hang up a lot when I run into them myself.

I'd just stowed Myra's tux in the closet when the phone rang. It was Philly Post.

"I'm flattered," I said when he identified himself.

"Don't be. It's business."

"I'm flattered even more." There was a long silence on the other end. It was obvious he didn't know what to think. "Did the FBI decide to take it?" I asked.

"Take what? What are you talking about?"

"Tucker said—"

"Tucker is an idiot. I checked with the feds on day one. They don't want this piece of shit any more than I do. Now, who did you say your little snitch was supposed to find?"

"Purdue?"

"Right."

"Lon Wilson."

"Are you sure?"

"Positive. Why?"

"Just stay right there. I'm sending a car to get you."

"What for?"

"I want you to come down to the station."

"I can drive down. I've got a car. What's this all about?"

"We'll talk here."

"Okay, okay. But don't send a car; I'll drive myself. I'll be there in fifteen minutes." Then I remembered the black-and-white. Even though I hadn't seen him since yesterday, he could still be around. "Better make it twenty."

* * *

He didn't exactly smile when I walked into his office, but he didn't glower at me like he had the times before. Progress. And his shirt wasn't pitted out so bad today.

"Sit down," he said.

"You mean I can stay?"

He actually chuckled. "Longer than you think."

At least when he was obnoxious, I knew where I stood. I settled into the chair and watched him with suspicion.

"Tell me about your conversation with Mr. Purdue." He shoved a stack of papers around to one side of his desk so he could see me when he sat down.

"I already told you about it. It's in the report your flunkie took down. Didn't you read it?"

"I want to hear it again. From you."

"Like I said, I followed August to a warehouse in Oakland. He met Purdue. They talked, then August drove away. I followed Purdue to his place and he told me August asked him to put the word out on Lon Wilson." I mustered a huge effort and smiled across the desk at him. "Do you want to tell me what this is about?"

"I've been giving some thought to what you said."

"You mean you're willing to listen to me?"

"I *am* listening," he said. "Talk."

"Not until you level with me. Something happened. Either last night or this morning. Something that made you realize I'm not just a crank."

The bushy brows all but obscured his eyes and his tone went flat. "We hauled Lon Wilson out of China Basin this morning."

"Drowned?"

He shook his head. "Sharp blow to the cricoid cartilage. Right here," he stretched his neck out and pointed to a spot just under his Adam's apple. "He was dead before he hit the water."

"Shit. Where was August?"

"Never mind August. August didn't leave his business card on top of Wilson's TV set. When did you talk to him?"

I glared. "Last night around nine o'clock."

"He got it around eleven, according to the report. Where were you then?"

He couldn't really suspect me. If he did, he would have had a black-and-white waiting for me when I got home instead of phoning me first and letting me drive in myself.

"I was in Spanish Heaven talking to a Mr. Martinez. And his aunt."

"Spanish Heaven?"

"It's a restaurant over in the Mission."

He took down Rogelio's number. "What did you and Wilson talk about?"

Blackie's warning about cops surfaced, but I pushed it aside. Philly Post played hardball, sure, and he was still all business, but something about him had changed. Maybe Blackie was wrong.

"I just asked him if Purdue had gotten in touch with him."

"What else?"

"Pete August's name came up."

Post didn't react. Another surprise. What *was* going on with him?

"What did he say?"

"No and no."

He stood. "I'm going to ask you to wait outside. Don't leave. I'll let you know when you can go."

I followed him to a bench outside in the hall, grateful that he hadn't arrested me—yet. It seemed a great act of self-discipline on his part, but then I didn't exactly know what was going on in his head. I'd thought he was hard to read before when he was just being a jerk. Now it was anybody's guess.

Thirty minutes later Post popped out of the door at the end of the hall and signaled me back into his office. I sat in the chair in front of his desk again while he stood about a foot away, his left hip hitched up against the front edge with his arms crossed and his brows crumpled ominously.

"Martinez confirmed your alibi, Ventana," he said. "You don't need a lawyer. At least not tonight."

He picked up a clipboard from his desk, jotted something on it, then set it down. "How well do you remember the last time we talked?"

"What do you mean?"

"I mean, didn't I tell you to stay out of this? Didn't I tell you I'd bust you for interfering?"

"Sure. But Wilson seemed pretty far removed from the Fort Point thing, at least according to you. And Purdue, well, you said they weren't even related."

"Yeah, right." He picked up the clipboard again and studied it. "Mr. Martinez said you asked him about Jake Murieta. What's Murieta got to do with any of this?"

"He's who August was really looking for."

Post looked skeptical. "Yeah?"

"Yeah."

After dropping the clipboard on the desk a second time, Post folded his arms across his chest and tucked his hands under his damp armpits. "Tell me something, Ventana. What makes you think any of this has anything to do with you? What do you care?"

"I saw a man killed. And the killer's still loose." He didn't say anything, and after a moment I glanced at my watch and stood up. "I've got to go," I said. "I've got Japanese tonight at six."

"Japanese?"

"Yes. Haven't you heard of it? It's a language."

19

On the drive out to City College, I kept telling myself that by this time next year I'd know enough Japanese to take on any high-tech industrial espionage-type cases that might come my way. Or at least that's how I had it figured. I was trying to gear my mind toward thinking Eastern thoughts for the rest of the evening, but instead the late Lon Wilson kept popping into my head.

He was a big man, and strong, but then so was August. August was perfectly capable of smashing Wilson's throat and throwing him into the Bay. *Was* it August again? I knew what he was capable of. I'd seen him in action. Why kill Wilson? Why Purdue? And why that poor little guy at Fort Point?

The key to their deaths had to be Jake Murieta. What did Murieta have or know that August would kill to find? What did it take to make August a killer? Whatever it was, I obviously hadn't found it yet. No, I had to find Murieta. He was the one with the answers.

I pulled off the highway onto Ocean Avenue and made

a right, then headed down the deep pit that was City's parking lot.

Over the next three hours I managed to forget Wilson and August and Murieta while I struggled with advanced Japanese grammar. If I never conquered the language, I told myself, at least I enjoyed the lessons, and the teacher gave out the name of a new sushi bar every week.

After class I threaded my way through the darkened parking lot and practiced saying *software* in Japanese. Before I knew it, Post was in my thoughts. He hadn't questioned August about Wilson's death, but it was only a matter of time before he'd have to. I hoped it wouldn't take another corpse to make him move on it.

It was weird he didn't seem upset that I was following my own leads. Maybe he was coming around. I shrugged. Cops. I'd never figure them out. Why try?

When I got near the car, I reached into my purse for my keys, then sensed, rather than heard, someone behind me. I looked over my shoulder. Nobody. Nothing. I was just spooking myself like I had the other night on the way to Wilson's house. I stuck the key in the door. This time I sensed something weird and *heard* it too.

I pivoted in time to see a dark shadow lunging right at me. The purse and books hit the ground at my feet just as the quick silhouette leaped forward. I raised my arms intending to deflect the attack by sliding sideways and using the attacker's own momentum to shove him past me, but it didn't work.

"Umph!" The charging body hit me full force, and we landed in a heap next to the Citroën's rear wheel. My back seemed to bounce off the pavement. I was surprised it didn't hurt more than it did. We scuffled around on the ground, grabbing at each other without doing much damage until I felt the punches. Quick, sharp karate jabs to my torso. Now *that* was pain.

"Ouch! Dammit!" I kicked my legs and managed to yank free, then scrambled to my feet. "Look, you," I shouted, hugging my side as I backed away.

He came at me again, like a dervish, menacing, arms and legs swirling.

"Hey! Hey, you there!" somebody shouted from somewhere behind us, and my attacker scurried away behind a row of parked cars. Between the hooded parka, the darkness, and what must have been a nylon stocking over his head, it was impossible to make anything out. But one thing was certain: Whoever it was was too small and too quick to be August.

I listened hard, tensed and barely breathing. But the only sound I heard was the hurried footsteps of some breathless student bounding across the lot to help me out.

"Are you hurt? I saw what happened. Did he get your purse?"

I took one look at the boy and had to hide my smile. He must have weighed all of ninety pounds. Coke-bottle glasses and pimples like a rash across both cheeks. Charlie Atlas he was not. Thank God for the cover of night. If my attacker had gotten a good look at him, he would have stayed to finish us both off.

"I'm fine," I said, pressing along each of my ribs to see if any hurt more than the others. They felt bruised but not broken.

I accepted the purse and books he picked up and handed to me. He was still breathing hard, excited.

"Are you going to report it? I'll be your witness. I saw it."

I unlocked my car and threw the stuff inside. "Tell you

what. You give me your name and phone number and I'll give it to the police."

His face fell. "Oh." But he told me his name and address anyway and made me repeat his number twice. I scribbled it down on the back of my Japanese workbook and left him staring forlornly at the back of the Citroën as I pulled out of the parking lot and drove straight to the Hall of Justice.

20

"**S**o you were mugged." Philly Post was unimpressed. "You've got the wrong department. This is Homicide."

"It wasn't a mugging. He didn't even try for my purse. It was me he was after."

Post looked up from a folder he'd picked up from the stack on his desk. "So what? You scared him off. You said he was little. He probably figured he bit off more than he could chew. It's that simple."

Something had changed since I'd seen him four hours earlier. He hadn't exactly been friendly then, but at least he'd been civil. Now he was acting like I wasn't even there.

"Right," I said, but he just went back to reading his report. "I thought you'd want to know. I think it's related to the Fort Point thing."

He looked up again. "Ms. Ventana, if you don't stop feeding me these stupid leads and telling me how to do my job, I'm going to pop you for interfering with an investigation."

"I don't get you, Post. First you refuse to believe me, then you treat me like your star witness, and now we're back to this again. What gives?"

The flat light from the ceiling made him look sallow. His longish hair was uncombed and he looked like he'd been sitting at that same messy desk for the past week.

"Why are you jerking me around?"

He got up and closed the door, then sat back down again. "You're the one who's fucking with me, Ventana," he said. "Is this your idea of fun?"

"Me? What are you talking about?"

"You really want to know?" He leaned forward, elbows on his desk, chin jutting out belligerently. "You want to know? I'll tell you. Thanks to you I hauled August in tonight for questioning on Wilson."

"That's great!"

He slammed the folder shut. "Great, huh? You've single-handedly killed my career. I was up for a promotion. Now I'm dead in the water, thanks to you."

"Why? What happened? What'd he say?"

"He's got an alibi. Know who he was with at eleven o'clock last night? His brother-in-law."

"So? There's got to be a way around that. They both must be lying."

Post's eyes were like ice. "Do you know who you're talking about?"

"August. And August's brother-in-law. Haul them both in and—"

I stopped. Philly Post's face had turned a deep purple and his thatched eyebrows dropped even lower. Here was the Post I knew—and loathed.

"Do you happen to know who married Peter M. August's sister?" he asked with a dangerous calm.

I clamped my eyes on his. He couldn't frighten me, no matter how self-controlled he tried to be. "God?"

"That's pretty damn close. Judge Herbert Marks."

My heart sank. "Maximum Marks?"

"Right. And if you don't—"

The light tap on the door behind me made us both jump. I was glad for the distraction. Maybe Post's blood pressure would drop a few notches if he thought about something else. This August business obviously wasn't too healthy for him to dwell on. Besides, I needed the time to think.

"Lieutenant, I'm sorry to interrupt." It was Kendall, the browbeaten but efficient officer who'd taken my statement the first time I came in.

"What is it?"

"A floater just washed up at Pier 45. Could be that victim from Fort Point."

Post's color came back. Hope transformed his face back into something human.

"Does the Captain know?"

"Not yet. I—"

"Great. Tell him about it. Tell him I went to check it out." He stood up, grabbed the jacket from his chair, then seemed to remember me. He fixed me with an ominous stare. "This better be it, Ventana, or you're dead meat."

I got to my feet. "Want me to come along?"

"Of course I want you to come along. How else are we going to I.D. the son of a bitch?"

"I'll come on one condition. If it's him, you've got to arrest August."

Philly Post froze at the door with one arm through the jacket's sleeve and the other behind his back. He stared at me like he thought I was crazy, then his stern face spasmed and he burst into a hearty, open mouthed laugh. He laughed hard and solid for a full minute, then let it fizzle into a slow chuckle. Poor Kendall just gaped.

"You have got the most balls of any woman I've met," Post said.

"I'll take that as a compliment, Lieutenant Post."

"Come on, Ventana," he said, slipping his arm through the other sleeve. "Let's see what they've got."

21

Ten minutes put us at Pier 45, just east of Aquatic Park. A few tourists meandered over the streets, diehards who wanted to eke out every minute of fun they could during their San Francisco holiday.

"Ever seen a floater?" Post asked as we left the car at the curb, its red strobe pulsating to match the tempo of the neon glitter along the wharf.

"Not exactly." I didn't intend to reveal that the man who blew his brains out in Italy was the first real dead person I'd seen. I hadn't been allowed to see my parents, and I didn't count my great-grandmother and Gran. They'd been laid out nicely and had looked pale and dead, but human. The guy in Italy hadn't.

We picked our way past a crowd of onlookers, then dropped off the pavement and made our way over rough rocks past the yellow tape the cops had draped around the scene, toward a set of bright spotlights that cut the night. There, by the water, a cluster of men huddled over something on the ground.

I didn't hurry. If it was the same man I'd seen go into

the Bay on Monday, he'd been in the water for four days. Four days with the fish and algae. Maybe I shouldn't have volunteered so quickly. Maybe it would have been better to let somebody else do the I.D. But who? I was the only witness and the only person insisting anything had happened in the first place.

I hung back behind Post and avoided looking where everybody else was looking. I was glad it was night.

Post walked up to a tall, loose-jointed man in an Oakland A's jacket and called him Brown. He seemed to be in charge.

"Think he's your man?" Brown asked.

"What do you think? Hey, Ventana, get your tail over here." The cluster parted, and Post pulled me into their center. Pointing to the sodden mass at our feet, he demanded, "Is it him?"

I glanced down. The thing at my feet didn't have a nose anymore. And what was supposed to be his skin was sort of purple and funny-looking.

That was enough. My stomach lurched and my throat constricted. I didn't even have to think about it, I knew I was going to vomit. I had barely enough time to push my way out to the water's edge before I threw up. Bent over, I retched, and then I retched again. For some reason I just couldn't stop. My poor bruised ribs ached with every spasm. Between heaves I heard somebody snicker.

"Oh, God," I gasped, wiping my mouth on my sleeve.

"Want this?" I looked up. It was Post. "Here. Use this." He dangled a plaid handkerchief under my nose.

I straightened myself up, met his eyes, then shook my head. "Thanks, but you're too late."

He shrugged and stuffed it back into his pocket. "This your first stiff?"

I rubbed my sleeve absently, found it wet, and wiped

my hands off on my thighs. "Fourth." Counting Gran and my great-grandmother. I'd thrown up then too. I'd forgotten until just now. Funny what you repress.

Post looked like he didn't believe me, but he let it go. He glanced over his shoulder at the gang around the corpse. "So what's the story? Is that him?"

"I don't know. I didn't get that good a look at him before, and he doesn't even look human now."

"What about his clothes?"

"To tell you the truth, I didn't look at them."

"Do you mean now, or before?"

"Now." I swallowed and stepped away from the mess I'd made on the water's edge. Post touched my elbow.

"You don't have to look at him. We can have the coroner send his clothes over later."

"I'll look now." I wiped my face with my sleeve again. "I haven't got anything left to lose. Literally."

That seemed to satisfy Post. "Colors look darker when they're wet," he said as he led me back toward the group. "And we've got artificial light out here. You saw him in daylight. Remember that."

"Right, right." I reached the circle and tried not to feel like a jerk wimp for throwing up.

"Cover his face," Post said crisply, and I leaned down closer to see. A faint, fishy odor wafted up to my nostrils. My stomach lurched again, but I clapped my hand over my mouth and pretended to cough. Thank God, nothing came up. The dead guy'd been through enough already. He didn't need me to throw up all over what used to be his face. I concentrated on the wet mass at my feet. Blue windbreaker, tan slacks. I stepped back and looked away.

"That's what he was wearing," I said when Post cleared his throat beside me.

"Any I.D.?" Post asked the guy he called Brown.

"We'll verify his prints, but his wallet says Jay-cobo Murieta. Ever heard of him?"

"Sure, we've heard of him, haven't we, Ventana?" Post locked his eyes on mine.

"So you want this guy?" Brown seemed anxious to get rid of the corpse. Post's teeth flashed pink in the red glow of the strobe. He slapped Brown across the back.

"Yeah," he said. "I'll take him."

22

"**Y**our career still on the skids?" I asked. We were on our way back to the Hall, just me and Post. The sergeant who had come out with us stayed behind with the coroner's van.

"I think it just came up for air," he said.

"So are you going to arrest August now?"

"And just what am I supposed to pop him for?"

"Try murder. You've got a body and an eyewitness."

"You can't hang a man with that. Not August anyway."

"Why not?"

"He golfs with half the D.A.'s office and plays tennis with the other half. He dates judges, he's related to judges."

"That shouldn't count."

"Where've you been, Pollyanna? I could pop him, sure, but he'd be out in fifteen minutes. There isn't a single guy in the D.A.'s office who'd go to trial with what we've got. Murieta's a sleazebag. And if we throw in Purdue and Wilson, we could say August did the world a favor."

"Is that how you see it?"

He didn't answer.

"Does he have an alibi for Monday morning?"

"He says he was at work in his office."

"Alone?"

"Yeah."

"Any hints as to motive?"

He shrugged, and we rode along in silence a few blocks.

"That's the hang-up, isn't it?" I asked. "If you had a decent motive you could pin on him, you could take it to the D.A., couldn't you?"

"It'd have to be something solid, so solid they couldn't turn it down."

"Listen, I've got an idea. Let me work the case."

He stopped at a red light and glanced sideways at me. He looked like I'd just told him I was from Mars. "Jeezus Christ! Think I'm stupid? Somebody ought to lock you up."

"Just hear me out a minute. I saw August kill Murieta. His alibi stinks, and you've got a body now. If I can find a motive, a rock-hard one—"

"Like what?"

"I don't know, but if I find it, you could be back in the running for that promotion."

Post snorted. "It'd be my ass. The man's got pull in a million ways."

"That's all the more reason to let *me* do it. Nobody needs to know we're working together. If I don't find anything, it won't count against you. And if I do, you get the glory. It's a no-lose situation."

He drove another block in silence, not saying yea or nay.

"I bet he's got access to your files," I said. "Anything

you do, he'll know about. But he can't know what's off
the record, right? Let me look into it. I'll find a motive.
We can have a case that'll hold him as tight as cement.
Nobody'll turn it down."

"Huh!" He was thinking it over, I could tell. Something about it had to appeal to him.

"What do you get out of it?" he asked at last.

"The satisfaction of putting a guilty man behind bars."

"Yeah? What else?"

I hesitated. "If you could help me out, sort of, from
time to time . . ." I said, but he wasn't listening.

"That would show those assholes. But what's important is to get that guy off the streets." He shook his head.
"I never thought I'd say that about Pete August. The
legend."

"Can you question him again?"

"August? No way." He thought for a minute. "What
about?"

"Robert Purdue."

"Who cares about that scum? He's out of my jurisdiction anyway and he's not even a homicide. No way. The
Captain'd put me away for good." He slowed down as we
neared the Hall. "Your car down here someplace?"

"Over there." I pointed to the corner and he pulled up
beside it. "So, do we have a deal?"

He gave me a stern look. "I want you to keep me
posted on every move, got that? If you sneeze, I want to
know about it. And no B and E's. I mean it. Forget all
that burglar alarm crap. Anybody catches you doing a
second-story job on August or anybody else, I never met
you, lady. I never even heard of you. Got that?"

"No problem. If that's what you want, partner, that's
what you'll get. I'll be in touch."

He let me out and disappeared around the corner. I

unlocked my door, got inside, and whooped: "Yahoo! Police access, here I come!"

I drove to Bernal Heights, straight to Blackie's house. It was a run-down, ticky-tacky place, just one notch above a shack, with a sweeping view of Interstate 280 and the farmers' produce market. None of Blackie's four ex-wives had been able to pry him out of it, but none of them had tried too hard either. Blackie managed to keep it by promising them all his income. Then he basically quit working.

The lights were out, but I knocked anyway.

"Blackie! Blackie, open up!" I knocked harder, then tried the rickety doorknob. The door yielded and I stepped inside.

"Christ, Blackie," I whispered when I flipped on the light.

The place looked ransacked. Junk was all over the place. You wouldn't think anybody could live in such a mess, but there, surrounded by empty beer bottles, crumpled cigarette packs, overflowing ashtrays, and miscellaneous junk on every flat surface in the room, lay Blackie, sound asleep on the couch. He was wearing crimson boxer shorts and a T-shirt. Yellow rubber flip-flops dangled from his big toe. In his arms he cradled an empty bottle of J & B like it was a baby.

"Blackhand Coogan." I shook my head. "What am I going to do with you?"

He snorted, opened one bleary eye, then sat up and tried to focus. Automatically he reached for the pack of Winstons on the table. "Ventana, what the fuck are you doing here?"

"I've got to talk to you."

"Shit."

"That's what I said when I saw this room. Blackie, this is disgusting. How can you live like this? Why don't you get a cleaning service or something?"

"I do. They come twice a year."

"What do women say when you bring them here?"

"We go to their place." He lit his cigarette and blew smoke up at the ceiling. "What do you want to talk about, Ventana?"

I eyed the empty fifth. "Are you sober?"

"No."

"How about some coffee?"

"What time is it?"

"Eleven thirty. P.M. Do you have something clean I can boil water in?"

He rubbed the gray stubble on his jaw and stared straight ahead like he hadn't heard. Maybe he hadn't. I went into the kitchen, found a kettle and some instant coffee and a couple of clean cups. Five minutes later I came back out with a steaming mug in each hand.

"Drink this," I said, handing him one of the cups. With my free hand I cleared the debris off the chair opposite the couch. As I sat down, the ache in my ribs diminished to a dull throb. Blackie stubbed out his cigarette on the top of an empty beer can, then took a long, slow slug of coffee.

"Aah! That's good." He wiped his mouth with the back of his bare arm. "What's up, doll? What's so important I can't sleep through it?"

"Two things. First, somebody jumped me tonight, out at City after my Japanese class."

He squinted, eyed me up and down, and seemed satisfied I was all in one piece. "Getting hot. August?"

"That's what I thought, but he's too big. This guy was smaller."

"What about the cop who razzed you outside August's office? What's his name?"

"No. He was too burly. This guy was somebody totally new. Post wouldn't even consider it as being connected."

"Fuck Post. What does he know? You want to spend the night with Uncle Blackie, is that it?"

"Would you mind?"

He snorted. "Mind? Hell, no. I never turn down a doll's offer—unless . . ." He reached for another cigarette and lit it. "Say, where were you last night? Didn't I call you? That redhead had fangs on her. I was counting on you to bail me out. She had to be Shirley's twin."

I looked around the room. "You don't need me. Just bring her here. That'll get rid of her."

"Yeah, well . . ." He contemplated the room as if seeing it for the first time. "Maybe that's what I did. I can't remember. But if I see her again, that's exactly what I'll do." He rubbed his chin with the cigarette hand, then sipped at his coffee again. "You can have that chair or the floor," he said. "The couch is mine."

"When are you going to buy a bed?"

"When I need one."

"How about a blanket?"

He pushed himself off the couch and tottered to a closet in the back, then came back a minute later with an old Indian blanket, folded and smelling of cedar. He set it down on the arm of the chair and sat back down to nurse his coffee and smoke.

"What else? You said there were two things. Let's hear the rest. I'm sober now."

"It's Post. He took me down to Pier 45 tonight."

"Let me guess. A floater turned up and it's your man."

"Jake Murieta. Have you ever heard of him?"

"Sure." He started to stub out his cigarette like he had

the first one, but changed his mind and held on to it. He propped his head up on his fist, elbow on his naked, knobby knee. "He's a two-bit piece of shit. No big loss. So Philly took you along, heh?"

"Strange, isn't it?" I watched Blackie blow the last of his smoke into the room. "Why do you hate him so much?"

"He's a piss ant jerk. Ain't that enough?"

"Come on, Blackie. I know you've got your reasons. What'd he do to you?"

"What the hell." He finished his coffee and leaned back against the couch. "I was doing a fucking runaway a few years back, maybe ten. The kid I was supposed to find got mixed up with some Polk Street asshole pimp and I talked the asshole into letting the kid go. Next thing I know Post nails me for assault and battery and kidnapping. If the kid hadn't backed down, I woulda done time. I'd be on parole right now." He lit another cigarette, took one drag, then stubbed it out. "Post is an asshole. He doesn't like how I operate. Now, you . . . now there's something different. He's sweet on you, Ventana. You'd better look out. In a couple of weeks he'll be begging to tell you all about his police business, just like your little buddy Aldo."

He chuckled, but when I smiled, he narrowed his eyes. "God save us. You didn't." He sat up and stared at me. "Shit, Ventana! How the fuck . . . ?"

"Post and I are partners. As of tonight."

He pursed his lips and whistled. "You're something, kid. I know you didn't sleep with him. How'd you do it?"

"He's a sensible man," I said. "He knows it's to his advantage."

Blackie laughed. "Jeezus! Listen to that crap! 'A sensible man.' Christ, he'd better hold on to his coin, 'cause you'll talk him out of that next. What's your side of the bargain?"

"Post needs a motive to lock in a solid case against August. His boss won't let him, but I can do it."

"So you're going to find out why a big-time private eye like August would bump off a little snitch like Gummy Purdue, a deadbeat like Wilson, and a two-bit act like Jake Murieta?"

"Exactly. If I were August and I wanted Murieta taken out, I'd hire somebody to do it, wouldn't you?"

"Sure."

"So why didn't he?"

"You got me. But I've got a feeling you're going to find out." He chuckled. "You know what Post's problem is? He's working with only half the brains you've got."

"I don't know, Blackie. I think maybe you're being a little too hard on him."

His bleary eyes narrowed, then his haggard face broke into a smile. "Don't pull my leg like that, Ventana. One of these days I'll believe you."

I laughed, then took the mugs back to the kitchen and rinsed them. Back in the living room I picked up the blanket and wrapped myself up in it, then checked out the floor. "You want me anywhere in particular?"

He waved his hand. "Anyplace is good." He pointed to an open space between the couch and the table. "You got some room there. You thrash around a lot?"

"Not like you do." The last time I'd stayed over at Blackie's he'd fallen off the couch three times. Each time he'd crawl back up and fall sound asleep again.

"Gotta get my fuckin' exercise some way," he'd said when I asked him about it the next morning.

I curled up between the coffee table and the door, propped my purse under my head for a pillow, and closed my eyes. "Good night, Blackie. Will you get the light?"

I didn't even hear him cross the room.

23

I was up and gone before the sun came up. I left a note for Blackie thanking him, kissed him on the forehead, and left him sleeping like a baby on the couch. He'd only fallen off twice during the night—that I'd counted.

The light on my answering machine was blinking. Whoever had called could wait. First things first. I ran five miles to work the stiffness out of my ribs, showered and dressed, then put on the Mr. Coffee, rewound the tape, and listened.

Someone had called all right—about four times—but there was no message on the tape, only dial tones and machine-generated beeps. Over coffee and a bowl of Cheerios I thought things over.

I had one dead body and a killer, but no motive. That was Jake Murieta. With Robert Purdue the motive could have been that August wanted to cover his tracks. He didn't want Purdue telling anyone he'd talked to him. But Purdue wasn't even on the books as a homicide, and to be perfectly objective, it could have been an accident.

Purdue really could have forgotten to stock a refill. Then there was Lon Wilson. That was anybody's guess. Besides, August had an alibi for that one.

There was always the remote possibility that the three murders weren't even related. But they were all strung together too neatly to consider that for long. The only murder Post could possibly pin on August right now was Murieta. But without a motive they'd never hold him.

The weirdest part was somebody trying to nail me at City. If it wasn't just a simple mugging—and I doubted that it was—then August had an accomplice. But why would he use an accomplice for me when he had killed Murieta on his own?

It didn't make sense. But then none of it did. According to Post, August wasn't even the type for homicide in the first place.

I stared out my window to the second-story window across the street. A Chinese woman was draping her family's wash along the sill to dry in the sun. I watched her lay out a couple of shirts and had just poured myself another cup of coffee when the phone rang.

"Come to Murieta's house," the caller whispered.

"Who is this?"

"Shhh. Come now." Click. The connection broke and the phone hummed in my ear. I replaced the receiver, poured the coffee back in the pot, and headed out the door. I'd been wondering where to start.

When I rang the bell at Murieta's house, it was close to noon. The police had had time enough to chat with the family and clear out, but I'd checked the street for unmarked cars before I stopped just the same.

While I waited, my eyes wandered to the unobtrusive crucifix above the door. I wondered if Murieta's wife would give him a church funeral and whether it'd be a good thing to go or not.

Before I could decide, however, the door opened and I found myself staring into the enormous black eyes I'd seen from deep inside the hall the day before. They belonged to a slender girl of about fifteen. Her long black hair was spiked on top, her eyelids were painted iridescent green, and she was wearing an oversized sweater, a tight miniskirt, and little gray boots. The scared look from yesterday was gone; today she looked hard and knowing.

I smiled and said hello with what I thought would be the proper decorum for a daughter whose father had just died. The girl didn't smile back.

"I'm Ronnie Ventana. I talked to your mother yesterday. Is she home?"

"My aunt." Her spunky voice was deep and sounded older than she looked. "She's not my mother, she's my aunt. My father's sister." The clarification seemed important to her, so I nodded.

"Your aunt, then. Is she home?"

"No." The girl shifted her weight to the other foot and leaned a narrow shoulder against the doorframe. "You asked about Uncle Jake yesterday. He's dead."

"I know. I'm sorry to hear that." The girl shrugged. It had taken a minute to sink in, but I was certain now. "You called me, didn't you?"

"Yeah."

"Why?"

"I want to know what you want. Why are you asking about Uncle Jake?"

I hesitated. "I'm trying to make a case against the man who killed him. I was hoping your aunt could help by telling me about your uncle and his friends."

"Why?"

"I saw him killed," I said.

The wide eyes blinked, sparkling green radiance at me. "Oh." She didn't even ask how, or why. "My aunt wouldn't tell you anything anyway. She's a hypocrite. Right now she's crying her eyes out at my grandmother's. And in her heart of hearts she's just as glad as I am he's dead."

"Oh?"

"He was a shit. He beat her. He beat everybody, everybody except Noni. If you ask me, we're all better off. I'm just sorry I didn't get to shove him in myself. My aunt is free now. That has to make her happy. It does me." Her grim smile was scary.

"Who's Noni?"

"His girlfriend. He was scared of hittin' her 'cause she's not Chicana. He treated her special."

"Do you think she'll talk to me?"

The girl shrugged. "I don't know."

"Where can I find her?"

"She works at the makeup counter at Manion's, downtown. High-class," she sniffed. "I think she's a hooker on the side."

"Did you hear me describe the man I asked your aunt about?"

She nodded.

"Have you ever seen your uncle talk to anybody who looks like that?"

"I can't remember," she said. "I don't think so. I mostly followed him over to see Noni. He was a real dodo about her."

"Is that why you called?" I asked. Since I'd been so slow to figure out she was the one who phoned me, I wanted to make sure I wasn't missing anything else.

"Are you kidding? I just wanted to know what you're doing. If you find out who did it, tell me so I can give him a prize." A phone rang somewhere down the dark corridor. She glanced over her shoulder, then back at me, flashing green when she blinked. "I guess I'd better get that. Good-bye," she said, and closed the door.

24

Noni, not surprisingly, wasn't at work. She'd called in, hysterical, and left the message that she'd had a personal tragedy and would try to come in the following day. Her supervisor was annoyed and told me so, but she wasn't annoyed enough to tell me where Noni lived. She did make the mistake of mentioning her last name, though. It was Witherspoon.

The phone book listed her as N. Witherspoon, no address. I called her from a pay phone in the fifth-floor lounge section of Manion's.

"Yes?"

The voice was tight, high-pitched, and strained. Whoever it was had been crying.

"Miss Witherspoon?"

"Yes?"

"I'm sorry to call you at such a bad time, but I—"

"Who are you? Are you with the press?"

"My name's Ronnie Ventana. I'd like to talk to you, please. It's pretty urgent."

"Are you a reporter? I don't—I can't—"

"I'm a private investigator, Miss Witherspoon. I've got to talk to you about Mr. Murieta."

"I really can't. Not now."

"Please, Miss Witherspoon. I was a witness to Mr. Murieta's death."

She paused, then sighed. "All right. Do you know where I live?"

She gave me a Diamond Heights address and, fifteen minutes later, let me into her fourth-floor apartment. Security-wise the place was an easy mark: lots of glass, and flimsy locks on the doors and windows. Anybody with a rope ladder could drop down onto the balcony from the roof and be inside within seconds. Probably because she was on the fourth floor, she figured she was safe. Either that or she was just used to being taken care of.

The view of the city's skyline and of the Bay was more than any cosmetics-counter girl could ever afford. Either Jake had helped her out or Murieta's niece was right about her being a hooker.

"I made some tea," Noni Witherspoon said, looking more composed than she'd sounded over the phone. Her makeup was in place, and her eyes, if not clear, at least were dry. "Would you like some?"

"Sure, that'd be nice."

I picked a soft beige tub chair with its back to the window and studied the woman across from me as she poured tea into gold-rimmed china cups. She was elegant and blond, with a model's graceful, long-limbed slenderness. I wondered what such a chic-looking lady would see in a thug like Murieta.

"I'm sorry to intrude on you like this," I began.

Noni smiled. "The police have already been here. You couldn't be any worse than they were." Her red-rimmed eyes studied me with a reluctant curiosity. "You saw it happen?"

"I'm afraid so."

"And you told the police?"

I nodded.

"They said he was a big man, white, not Mexican, and that he's got a streak of blond or white in his black hair. Is that right?"

"Yes."

"Why haven't they found him? He sounds like he'd stick out like a sore thumb."

"Miss Witherspoon—"

"Please, call me Noni."

"—Noni. I'm sort of looking for him too. Did you ever see Mr. Murieta associate with anybody fitting that description?"

She looked past me to the skyline. "They said he was knocked out and thrown in the water. Is that what happened?"

"Yes."

"Jake knew how to swim, Miss Ventana. He was an excellent swimmer. The best. If he'd been conscious, he—he'd—" She pulled a handkerchief from her pocket and dabbed at her eyes. She even cried elegantly.

"Miss Witherspoon—Noni—did the police talk to you about a possible motive?"

"They asked me if Jake had enemies. How am I supposed to know? I told them no. He never talked about any."

"Would he? I mean, talk to you if there were."

"I think he would."

"Did he talk much about his, er, work?"

"Sometimes."

"Did he ever mention the name Pete August?"

"The investigator? No."

"If he'd met August, would you have known about it?"

She smiled and crumpled her handkerchief in her hand. "Sure. I know Jake. He's a name-dropper." She gnawed at her lip. "I mean, he *was*. If he'd had anything at all to do with Pete August, he would have told me." She looked sad but beautiful. "He liked to impress me."

"When was the last time you saw him?"

"Sunday morning. He came over for breakfast after he dropped his wife off at church. That's usually how our Sundays went."

"Did he talk about his work then?"

Noni poured out more tea and seemed to think for a while. "Not really. We talked about a lot of things, but business, no."

"What exactly did he do for a living?" I asked.

"A little bit of everything. People were always calling him up and asking him to do things."

"What sort of things?"

"Find people, talk to people. Probably like what you do," she said.

Sure. "And you're certain he never mentioned August?"

"No. Is he working on it too? Jake did some work for a judge every now and then, but that's as close as he got to working with the law."

"A judge? Who? Was it Marks? Maximum Marks? Herbert?"

Noni shook her head and stared out the window again, her pale, beautiful face a study of grief.

"I'm sorry," she said after a moment. "It could have been. I don't know . . . I'm just so . . . so . . ." She covered her face and started sobbing. I stood up and patted her shoulder.

"I understand. Thank you, Miss Witherspoon, Noni, for talking to me. If you think of anything that might help, like the judge's name, will you call me? Here's my card."

Noni reached long, taloned fingers out and took it without looking up. "I'm sorry," she sobbed. "I just can't—"

"That's all right, I understand. I'll see myself out."

25

"**Y**ou want me to do what?" Blackie leaned across the table in the Quarter Moon Saloon below my apartment and lowered his voice against the early-afternoon crowd. "I'm not breaking into any judge's office."

"Chambers, Blackie. They call them chambers. It'll just take a couple of hours," I said. "I wouldn't ask, but it's a two-man job. The Hall of Justice is a pretty tight place."

"It ought to be. It's a fucking jail, Ronnie. Police headquarters!" He frowned, shook his head, and lit a cigarette.

"He's got to be the judge Noni was talking about. It's *got* to be him. He's August's brother-in-law."

"What do you think you're going to find—a signed confession?"

"Don't be rude, Blackie. Marks is tied to this thing. He's got to be. I just don't know how."

He shook his head. "Somebody's house, maybe, or a place of business, but a fucking judge's office in a fucking jail? For crying out loud, get your head out of your ass,

Ventana. You're good, but you're good at busting alarms.
There ain't no security alarm at the Hall of Justice. You
know why? 'Cause they got so many cops swarming
around, they don't need one. Think about it, doll. What
you're good at ain't no good for this job."

"All right, all right. We'll do his house, then."

Blackie pushed his beer mug to one side and blew
smoke into the already smoke-filled air above our heads.
"Breaking and entering is something they bust you for. It
ain't something you want to do just 'cause you got a
hunch about somebody. You don't do it unless you absolutely fucking have to."

"Well, I absolutely have to."

"No, you don't."

"Blackie, I—"

"Talk to your buddy Post. He's got to be good for
something."

"I don't want to talk to him just yet."

"He could drop you a lead, doll. That's all you need."

I didn't say anything.

"What's the matter? Afraid he'll call it off if he sees
how big it's getting?"

He rounded the burning ash off the end of his cigarette
by swirling its tip against the bowl of the ashtray. When
he'd finished, he looked up and waited.

"Something like that," I said.

"Shit, use Aldo, then."

"Aldo?"

"Sure. Why not?" He took a quick, powerful drag
from his cigarette, stubbed it out, and let the smoke waft
out between his lips while he spoke. "You want scut-
tlebutt, gossip, anything that could put you on to something. He can't have worked there as long as you say he

has without hearing something on old Maximum Marks." He drained his beer. "What do you say?"

"It's worth a try, I guess. But if he doesn't pan out, will you help me do the judge?"

Blackie gave me a sour look. "Dammit, Ventana. Did you hear anything I said?"

"Sure. I'm calling Aldo first, aren't I? Now, do you want in on the judge, or not?"

"His house," he said. "No chambers."

"No chambers."

"Dammit, Ventana. All right, I'll consider it."

26

"I never knew you had your own office, Aldo. This is nice."

The room was simple and cramped but private, furnished in early city government exactly like Post's office, except this room was kept neat and tidy under the watchful, glassy eyes of a big, gape-mouthed trout glued to a plaque on the wall.

"It's my boss's," Aldo said. "He's on vacation until Monday. I'm acting chief of administration, so I get to sit in here."

"I guess he likes to fish, huh?" I asked.

Aldo followed my eyes to the trophy on the wall behind him, then grinned. "Yeah. He's from Montana. That's where he is right now—fishing."

"Think he'll bring back another one?"

"I wouldn't be surprised."

"Mind if I close the door? I need to talk to you. It's sort of confidential."

"Go right ahead." He seemed pleased that I'd come to him. "But if you want me to check out some felon for you, Ronnie, I'm sorry. I just can't do that anymore. It was a bad idea. I never should have offered to start doing that in the first place." He wasn't angry, just firm.

"That's all right," I said, and sat down. "I wasn't going to ask you to."

"Good. You understand, don't you? It's just not a good idea anymore."

"Sure, sure. Don't worry about it." I leaned forward conspiratorially, my forearms resting against the edge of the desk like I was going to let him in on some great big secret. "I came to see you about something else."

He was loving it, so I leaned even closer.

"It's about Judge Marks," I whispered.

"Judge Herbert Marks?" His face scrunched up. I could tell he was starting to get mixed up already. "What about him?"

"That's what I need to know. What can you tell me about him?"

"Ronnie, I just told you—"

"He's not a felon, Aldo. Besides, I don't want police records, I just want to know what's the latest office gossip, that's all. Please, Aldo."

His bland face went back to its normal shape again when he narrowed his eyes at me. "Are you going after Judge Marks?"

"Not exactly. But he could be tied into this mess."

"What mess?"

"The Pete August thing."

He looked incredulous.

"It's just a hunch, Aldo, but it needs looking into."

"I don't know, Ronnie." He looked around the room, then back at me. He was nervous. "I'm not real comfortable talking here."

"Aldo, please don't ask me to lunch. I can't wait that long. Not this time."

"Do you know what you're doing, Ronnie? Do you realize what you're asking me to do? Pete August is pretty high up there. But Judge Marks, he's like an institution around here."

"I know, I know. That's why I came to you, Aldo. This is important. I need some reliable stuff on the guy."

"Post will—"

"Don't worry about Post," I told him. "I promise he won't know. And even if he did, you wouldn't have to worry. I promise."

"How can you—?"

"Don't ask me to explain, Aldo. I've said too much already."

"Yeah?" He picked up a pencil and tapped the desk with it. "I don't know, Ronnie."

"All right. How about if I tell you what I know and you tell me if I get off track?"

From the look on his face, he was wavering. At least he hadn't said no yet. I dove in before he could.

"I know Marks and August are related. They're in-laws, right?"

Aldo nodded.

"Who married who?"

Aldo hesitated.

"Come on, Aldo, help me out here."

"Judge Marks married August's sister."

"When he was working in the D.A.'s office?"

Aldo nodded again. "He quit a couple of years later when Judge Marks got his appointment to the bench."

"And that's when August opened up his own agency."

"Right."

"Are the two of them in on anything together? Business? Hobby? Anything like that?"

"Oh, no. They're barely on speaking terms anymore."

"Why? What happened?"

"The sister. About three years ago something happened. She went crazy. August didn't like how the judge handled it. Judge Marks went over his objections and institutionalized her. They've hardly said a word to each other since. I think they go together to see Mrs. Marks once a week and they must talk then, but I saw them pass in the hall last month when August testified on a case and they didn't even look at each other."

"And the sister?"

"Nobody talks about her. She's in a nuthouse down the Peninsula."

"Mmm. People don't just lose it for no reason. What flipped her out?"

Aldo straightened a stack of reports on a corner of the desk and avoided looking at me. He picked up the pencil again and fidgeted.

"What else, Aldo?"

"It's just gossip, Ronnie. It's not reliable information like you want."

"Everything's important, Aldo. I'll take it with a grain of salt—unfounded gossip."

"Well . . ."

"Yes?"

"They said it was rape. That's what made her go bonkers. Judge Marks didn't do anything about it, finding the rapist or anything like that. August wanted to, but Judge Marks wouldn't let him. He refused to cooperate and acted like nothing had happened."

"Why?"

Aldo shrugged. "Who knows?"

I sat back in my chair. "How'd you find out about this?" He'd given me far more than I'd expected.

Aldo blushed. "I was dating Judge Marks's secretary when it happened."

"Yeah? Then it's pretty reliable. What asylum did he put her in?"

"Some place in Redwood City. Green something."

"What else?"

"About Judge Marks? Nothing. Except that he's the toughest judge in the state. The D.A. loves him, and so does every police officer in the city. Any felon that stands trial before him is sunk."

"I always heard that," I said. "It's true, huh?" He nodded. "Are you sure you haven't heard any rumors about Marks lately? Anything dark and sinister that could link him up to some crime or criminal. You know, some scandal-type stuff?"

He dropped the pencil on the desk. "Of course not! Ronnie, what does any of this have to do with August committing homicide at Fort Point?"

I stood up. "You know, Aldo, that's a real good question. I'm not quite sure of the answer, though, and that's why I'm trying to figure it out. It's just a hunch I'm playing."

"Dammit, Ronnie. Excuse the language, but you do this to me every time."

"What?"

"Pump me for information, then leave me high and dry."

"Don't pout, Aldo. It doesn't look dignified. Especially in your boss's office."

"Aren't you going to tell me?"

"There's nothing to tell."

"Ronnie—"

"I've got to go, Aldo. I'll see you later."

From the pay phone in the lobby downstairs I called Information and got the number for Greenside Convalescent Home in Redwood City.

27

I dropped two dimes in and dialed. A pleasant female voice answered at the other end.

"I need to speak to someone regarding Mrs. Marks. Mrs. Herbert Marks," I said.

"Just one moment. I'll connect you with Dr. Taft's office."

A half second later a different voice came on the line. "Dr. Taft's office."

"Good afternoon," I said. "I'm sending a letter to Dr. Taft and I need the correct spelling of his full name."

"Of course. That's Albert. A-L-B-E-R-T. Taft. T-A-F-T."

"Very good. Will he be in at four o'clock this afternoon? I'll hand-deliver it if he is."

"I'm afraid the doctor will be out of the office after four. You can leave it at the front desk, though. They'll make sure he gets it."

I hung up, got no answer at Blackie's, so tried the Quarter Moon Saloon. He wasn't there either. As a last resort I dialed Mitchell's office and thumbed to the doctor listings in the yellow pages while the phone rang. Mitch picked up his private line after the third ring.

"Mitchell, listen, can you do me a favor?"

"Ronnie?"

"Right. I'll bring your car back in a couple of days, okay? I'm being careful with it."

"No rush."

"Good. Will you answer your private line for the next couple of hours by saying—hold on a sec," I glanced down at the listings in front of me. "Say, 'Dr. Jack Basin,' all right? And if anybody asks, Judge Marks wants a second opinion on his wife."

"*Is* there a Dr. Jack Basin?"

"Yes. I've got the yellow pages right here. His name's actually John, but a lot of Johns go by Jack." I paused. "Maybe you'd better write it down."

"I already have. Ronnie, we have to—"

"Is this about that job?"

"Yes. Skipper really wants to talk to you."

"Mitchell, I've got a job. Two in fact. I don't need another one. Listen, tell Skipper thanks, okay? I've got to go, but I'll be in touch. Remember—Dr. Jack Basin."

Next I drove home and pulled a white smock out of my closet. Forty minutes later I pulled up in front of Greenside Convalescent Home and made a beeline for the front door.

It was after four o'clock, and inside the building's double glass doors the clinic was bright, open, and inviting. A skylight over the front desk lit the foyer and let in enough sun to grow the minijungle of plants that lined the inside walls. It was quiet and clean, not a bad place. If I lost my mind and had to veg out my life, I wouldn't mind vegging it out in a spot like this.

The receptionist behind the desk was something else,

though. I couldn't have asked for a better mark. She looked so ditzy for a minute I wondered if they let the patients work the desk. Her black hair was piled up on top of her head in a tumble of frizz with—I had to look twice to make sure—half-dollar-sized fake butterflies dotting the whole mess. She was on the phone when I walked in and her voice sounded friendly, though it could have been a personal call for all I knew. When she looked up, I grinned and hoped for the best.

"Hi! I'm Janet from Dr. Basin's office."

The butterflies quivered. She gave me a blank look. So far, so good.

"I'm here to pick up the file from Dr. Taft. Did he leave it with you?"

"A file? Whose file?" Maybe she wasn't as goofy as she looked.

"Mrs. Herbert Marks."

"Hmmm, let me see." She punched a few keys of the computer on the desk, and for a minute I thought one of the butterflies was going to fall out of her hair, but it stuck. She smiled. "Here she is. Chelsea Marks." She touched another button and a printer against the back wall snapped into action. "There we go." She turned back to me. "Funny, he didn't say anything before he left."

"Well, I didn't exactly talk to him myself. Dr. Basin arranged it."

"Oh. That explains it. They don't know who *really* run their practices, do they?" I smiled but couldn't take my eyes off the printer. It was chattering along, just spewing out the report. All right! I hadn't expected it to be this easy.

"It'll take a few minutes to print the whole thing out," she said.

"That's okay, I don't mind. Do you have a ladies' room I could use?"

"Down the hall on your left."

"Thanks."

I walked down the hall, reading the patients' names marked on each of the doors, hoping to find Mrs. Marks, but I didn't have any luck. When I went back to the desk, the printer was silent, but the receptionist looked at me like she'd never seen me before. "May I help you?"

"Mrs. Marks. You were getting her file for me," I said.

"Mrs. Marks?"

I pointed to the printer behind the desk and suddenly it clicked for her. She laughed, and the butterflies danced in her hair. "Silly me." She tore the printout from the machine. "Here you go."

I reached across the counter, but before I could get my hands on it, some woman shouted from behind me.

"*What* are you doing, Miss Avalon?"

The butterfly lady stared past me. From the look on her face, I figured whoever it was, was pretty horrible. Her hand, the one with the report, jerked the pages back out of my reach. She smashed the papers to her chest and looked guilty. All I could do was shake my head and act like I didn't know what was going on, which wasn't too tough.

"Mrs. Grady. You scared me," the butterfly lady said. "I was just giving this file to Dr. Basin's secretary."

The squabby thing called Mrs. Grady slid behind the counter and glared at me. She was big and looked nasty, like she hated life and wanted everybody else to too. When I didn't waver, she went for the easy victim and stared Miss Avalon down. Then she thrust out her fat little hand. "May I see the release form?"

Miss Avalon squirmed. "I forgot to ask her for one."

She turned to me, looking pitiful and embarrassed. "Can I have it, please?"

"Do you really need one? I guess I forgot to bring it." I struggled to appear contrite.

"You what?" Mrs. Grady drew herself up. She had the eyes of a piranha. "*Whom* do you work for?"

"Dr. Basin."

"Get me that phone book." She pointed under the desk.

"His number's 567-8950," I said helpfully. Mrs. Grady started to reach for the phone, but goofy Miss Avalon put the telephone book under her nose. I wanted to kick her in the teeth. Grady picked up a pen.

"What's that number again?"

I told her and she wrote it down, then reached for the phone book.

"The numbers won't match," I said. "He's working at home today and his home number isn't listed."

Mrs. Grady snorted, slammed the book shut, and glared at me. "Who are you?"

"Dr. Basin's secretary."

"Whoever you are, you're not getting your hands on this printout without a release." Mrs. Grady held her hand out for the file, and Miss Avalon obediently handed it to her. The old battle-ax tore it in half and made a big show of dumping it in the trash behind the desk. "I don't care where your Dr. Basin's working, he can't have this file without a signed release from either the patient or her husband. That's policy and you should know it. Don't come back here without one."

Back in the parking lot I slouched down in the front seat and decided to punt. It was close to five, a quarter till in fact, and they had to be going home soon. I hoped they both got off at five.

But only dizzy Miss Avalon pranced out to her Datsun a few minutes after five. Grady didn't come out until half an hour later. I waited until the old shrew squeezed into her silver Dodge van and disappeared around the corner. Then I jumped out of the car and into the white smock I'd packed. I tied a bandanna around my hair and traded my purse for a big black garbage bag from the trunk, then, using my picks, slipped in the back door.

It was a straight shot to the reception desk from the rear door, so I headed up the hall, emptying the two little wastebaskets I passed along the way.

When I got there, the reception was deserted. It took me only a minute to empty the torn file into my bag. I tamped down the papers and started back down the hall.

"Hey you, wait a minute!"

I shuffled onward, dragging my bag.

"Wait up, there!"

When I turned around, a man in a guard's uniform was hurrying toward me. *Don't panic.* "Yeah?"

"Are you new?"

"Started yesterday."

"You forgot this one." He tapped a waste can next to one of the potted plants with his foot. I ducked my head down and shuffled over to empty it. He glanced down the hall. "Where's the rest of the crew?"

"They'll be by later."

The guard thought that over, then smiled. "What's your name, honey?"

"Janet."

"You're kind of cute, Janet. Anybody ever tell you that?"

"Only my two-hundred-pound linebacker husband," I said.

The guard looked at me funny, then he slapped his

thigh. "That's a good one, honey. Two-hundred-pound linebacker. Heh, heh. I like that. You had me going for a minute there." I started down the hall toward the back and he walked along with me. "I just want to welcome you aboard, honey. It's good to see a pretty face around. If you need anything, just ask for Tippy. That's me." He patted my butt and gave me a big broad wink. *"Anything at all."*

I stopped and looked him up and down. "I get off at midnight. Want to meet out back?"

That took him by surprise. "Uh—ah—uh, what?"

I winked up at him. "You're right. I can't wait that long either. How about in an hour? I get to take a break then."

He backed away, keeping his eyes on me the whole time like he'd surprised a tarantula. "I—uh—I'll have to get back to you on that, uh, Janet," he said. "Uh, right now, I've gotta do my rounds, check the doors and all."

He turned on his heel and tripped over his own big feet in his hurry to get away from me. I didn't stop laughing until I hit the Broadway Street off-ramp.

28

"**W**hat is this shit?" Blackie asked when I dumped the plastic garbage bag on the floor in the middle of my apartment. He'd been downstairs at the Quarter Moon when I walked by, so he came upstairs with me when I wouldn't stop to talk.

"This, my boy, is hard-earned evidence. You would have been proud of me." I searched through the rubble and told him how I'd gotten the file. When I finished, he chuckled out loud.

"You're dangerous," he said.

"Here. This is it." I pulled a stack out of the mess on the floor.

"You only want the top half? What the—?"

I fished out the bottom half, set the complete file on the table I used for a desk, and scooped everything back into the bag.

"Hand me that Dustbuster, will you?"

While Blackie watched, I vacuumed what was left on the floor, tied a knot in the bag, and dragged it over to the door.

"Nobody'll ever accuse you of chivalry," I said.

"It's your garbage, doll. Got a beer?"

"All out. Want to bring some up from downstairs?"

"If you're buying?"

"Sure." I pulled some bills from my wallet and listened to him totter down the stairs while I sat down at the table with a roll of Scotch tape. It took me only a couple of minutes to piece the report back together. Then I started to read. I didn't notice how long Blackie was gone, but when he came back, he only had three beers with him.

He plopped down on the sofa bed across from me. "What the hell's in that file?"

I didn't look up, but I wasn't reading anymore. I was just sitting there, staring at the printed page and feeling sick.

"What's the matter?" he said. "You don't look too good."

"I wish to God I hadn't taken it."

"What's so bad you need a conscience?" He walked around behind me to read over my shoulder. Then he whistled. "Jesus Christ. Where'd you get that shit?"

"I told you, Blackie. It's her official file. This is the doctor's report." I glanced up over my shoulder at him. I could smell the beer and tobacco on his breath and the musty, faded scent of his after-shave. "She was gang-raped, Blackie."

"I can fuckin' see that. What's catatonia?"

"Sort of a self-imposed coma."

"She's a vegetable?"

"Mentally. She's escaped into her own world. Someplace where nobody can hurt her." I stood up. "What'd you do with the beer?"

"It's over there." He pointed to the floor next to the couch and dropped into my empty chair. I popped the bottle open and sank onto the couch to watch Blackie's expression while he read the report.

"This is disgusting," he said. "I'm surprised she's still alive."

"She probably wishes she was dead."

He flipped back to the front page. "Maximum Marks, huh? Why didn't we read about this shit? How'd he keep something like this out of the fucking papers?"

"Aldo said they hushed it all up. That file says she couldn't testify even if they found the guys. I guess that's why Marks didn't pursue it."

"So these animals are loose?"

"That's what it looks like."

He shook his head again and turned back to the body of the report. "If anybody'd done this to my wife, I woulda hunted them down like animals. Nobody deserves this."

When he finished reading, he came over to sit next to me on the sofa bed. I handed him the last beer.

"What are you going to do now?" he asked after he downed half the bottle in one swig.

"I was looking for something to tie August and the judge to Jake Murieta."

"Yeah? You think Murieta was in on this?"

"It would give them both a motive to kill him."

"Come on, Ventana. Murieta's a hired killer."

"So? A killer could do something like that."

"These guys, they have code," Blackie said. "Rapists are at the bottom of the barrel. Rapists and child molesters."

"What are you saying?"

"I'm telling you that maybe not even Murieta would stoop to that kind of crime."

I rubbed my eyes with both hands. My whole body

hurt. "I don't know what to think, Blackie. I feel like throwing up." I thought of Noni Witherspoon, of Mrs. Murieta and of the swollen, fish-mauled corpse that was Jake Murieta. If he was guilty, then justice, in a way, was served. "Well, he's dead now." I finished my beer. "I'd better call Post." I reached for the phone.

"And tell him what? What are you going to tell him? How are you going to explain that file?"

"Blackie, he *told* me to look into the case. He's not going to bust me for checking things out for him."

"You sure about that?"

"He as much as asked me to. I've got to tell him about this."

"Why? What's it prove?"

I shrugged.

"I'll tell you what it proves, doll. It proves that the lady was raped by a bunch of animals and left for dead. That's all. It doesn't tie Murieta in to it. It doesn't even tie August or Marks to Murieta. Ventana, listen to me for a change. If you call Post, he's going to tell you you haven't got squat. And you know what? He'll be right."

As much as I hated to admit it, Blackie had a point. I didn't have anything. Short of showing Jake's picture to Mrs. Marks, I couldn't tie them together. And if Mrs. Marks couldn't testify three years ago, she probably couldn't do it now either.

"Come on, doll." Blackie stood up. "Let's go get something to eat."

"I'm not hungry, Blackie."

"Sure you are. Everybody's gotta eat, babe. Come on, let's go."

I reached for my jacket and the blinking red light on the telephone answering machine caught my eye. "Hold on a sec. I forgot to check my messages."

"Do it later. Let's get out of here."

We ended up having a liquid dinner. We stopped at the Quarter Moon downstairs, then walked down a block to Giano's, then two blocks to Tosca's, then across the street to Olympia's, where we ran into Blackie's son, Joey.

Somehow we ended up in an East Bay jazz club listening to somebody neither of us had heard before. It didn't matter. Mostly I just wanted to forget for a little while what had happened to Mrs. Marks. And by the time me and Blackie and Joey closed the club and made it back to the city, I was lucky to remember my name.

When I woke up at noon the next day, I decided to skip my run. It felt too early to move, much less run. I crawled off the sofa to the desk and called Blackie's to see if he'd made it home after dropping me off. The phone rang twenty-two times before he picked it up.

"Fuck off," he growled, then slammed the receiver down.

After a long shower and three cups of coffee, I remembered the phone machine. I pulled out a pad and pencil, rewound the tape, and played the messages back. Two Tuxedo Message calls, both for next week, a call from Mitch telling me he wasn't going to do the phone bit or any other crazy thing like that for me anymore ever again, and one from Philly Post ordering me to call him or he'd have me arrested.

I checked out the Tuxedo messages first, got things lined up to do them, then, after another cup of coffee, phoned Philly Post.

"So what's up?" I asked when he barked his name over the line.

"Who is this?"

"Your partner," I said. "Remember me?"

"Where the hell have you been?"

"Do you have to talk so loud? I kind of have a head-ache."

"Tough shit. I told you to keep me posted."

"Yeah? Want to know what I've been doing since night before last?"

"What?"

"Barking up the wrong tree. Look, I need to see you. I'd like to take a look at your file on Jake Murieta. Wilson and August, too, if there's anything there." I threw them in for good measure.

"You don't need to see that shit. You're supposed to be—"

"Don't be a chump, Post. How can I know what I'm doing if I don't know the history?"

"Don't push the limit, Ventana."

"Half an hour, that's all I need. Your office? Twenty minutes?"

He muttered something I chose not to understand and hung up. I figured he said yes, so I poured myself a last cup of coffee, drank it, and headed for the Hall of Justice.

29

The file the cops had on Murieta wasn't worth the trip down to the station. There were four pages in it. Period. Pete August's file was a single sheet with my statement stapled to it, and Lon Wilson's had a couple of priors and an autopsy report in it. I looked up across Philly Post's desk and scowled at him.

"This is it?"

"Read 'em and weep." He leaned back in his chair and linked his fingers behind his head. He looked less sallow today—maybe because he was wearing a red tie. I picked up Murieta's jacket and opened it to the first page. It was dated 1982.

"Looks like you guys are a little behind in your paperwork."

"Save it, Ventana. What have you got so far?"

I ignored him, scanning the page.

"What have you got?" he said again. I shut the folder and set the three files on his desk in a neat pile.

"I've got a couple of leads," I said.

"Let's hear them."

I took a deep breath. "You know, I've been thinking about that."

Post dropped his arms and leaned forward, eyebrows furrowed and threatening. "This better be good. Let's hear it."

"This is a real tricky situation we have here. I've been giving it a lot of thought. Do you *really* want to know? I mean, think about it. It might be better if you just get the bottom line, no details. That way if there's any problem —and I'm not saying there will be—but just in case, you'd be legitimately off the hook."

"The leads, Ventana."

"I really don't think it's a . . ." He pressed his lips together in a grim, rigid line and waited. The message was clear: no bullshit. "All right, all right. But before I say anything, I want you to remember you asked me to check this stuff out."

"Yeah, yeah," he said, "and I already regret it."

"Now, I want you to keep in mind that—"

"Talk, Ventana."

"All right. I checked out August's sister. Mrs. Maximum Marks."

"You what!" He shot out of his chair, huffing like an angry bull. "You're out of your league, lady. As of this minute, right now, you're off this case."

"Sit down," I said. "Let me finish. I needed to know what happened to her."

He clenched his teeth. "What do you mean 'what happened to her'?"

"It was a lead. I followed it. Don't get so excited." His face was as close to burnt sienna as I've ever seen on a human. He didn't look good at all. "Do you have high blood pressure or something? Maybe you ought to sit down."

He wasn't even listening. "All I need is for the Captain to find out I'm not just after Pete, I'm gunning for Marks too. Damn!" He glared at me, then narrowed his bushy brows. "What happened to her?"

I hesitated. He didn't look calm enough to hear what I had to say, but I figured I might as well get it all over with up front. "She was raped three years ago. It pushed her over the edge and now she's in an asylum."

Post shook his head. "No way. I would have heard about it."

"It happened in Oakland."

"I still would have heard."

"Not if Judge Marks didn't want anybody to know. He didn't press charges, and she wasn't in any shape to. Still isn't, as far as I can make out."

"How'd you find this out?"

"I got a look at her file."

He reached behind him, felt for his chair, and sat back down without a word.

"It's a motive," I said.

"Revenge?" He shook his head. "Not Pete's style."

"What exactly is his style?"

Post cocked his head and smirked. "All right. Say he took Murieta out because he raped his sister. Let's throw Lon Wilson in there too. And your little snitch, Purdue. Let's say it all went down the way you say it did. When did this happen?"

"June, three years ago."

Post riffled through the files I'd just put on his desk. "No go. Murieta was locked up then. So was your snitch." He tossed the open file under my nose and stood up. "Try some other angle, Ventana. Just leave Marks out of it."

I glanced down at the folder and something caught my

eye. I looked up, tapped the page with my index finger, and grinned. "Bingo," I said. "It's right here under our noses."

He rolled his eyes and flopped back into his chair. "What?"

"It's right here in black and white. There *is* a connection." I set the folder back on his desk and turned it around so he could read it. "Murieta stood trial before Marks. See? That *proves* they knew each other."

"Why? Why are you doing this to me?"

"Somebody said Murieta did some work for a judge. Hey, are you listening?"

"Okay, okay." He ran a hand over his face and looked up. "What'd you say? Somebody said Murieta did a hit for a judge?"

"Some 'work.' It wasn't anything as specific as a hit."

"And the tie-in is they met in trial?"

"Right. It's right there. Nineteen eighty-two. I'll have to talk to Murieta's attorney and see what he remembers about the trial, then—"

He raised his hand. "Just do it," he said. "You said more than I want to know already."

"Don't you want to hear what's next?"

Post closed his eyes and I could have sworn he shuddered. "Just do it. The less I know, the better."

I grinned and cocked a finger at him. "You're a smart man, you know that?"

"Tell it to the Captain."

30

"**T**hat's a hell of a thin connection," Blackie growled.

We were back at the Quarter Moon Saloon. The three-o'clock sun slanted across our table, warming our beers and my face.

"I know, I know. But it's all I've got for now since the Mrs. Marks thing didn't pan out and Murieta's public defender joined the Peace Corps. Zimbabwe isn't exactly accessible. Checking out Marks is the next logical thing on the agenda."

"You think he's going to leave something lying around the house just so you can come along, bust in, and fucking find it?" He lifted his mug and shook his head. "Ventana, sometimes I think I did wrong with you. Breaking and entering ain't supposed to be the party you make it out to be."

"Don't you like a challenge?" He didn't answer. Instead he reached for a smoke. I kept after him. "You're the best, Blackie, and the smartest thing you ever did was show me the ropes."

"Your folks did that."

"But you showed me how to be a P.I. A damn good one. You said so yourself."

"Wasn't sober."

"Just think about it, all right?"

He coughed as he lit his cigarette. "Hell, who are you kidding, doll? You're going in with or without me."

I grinned. Sometimes I thought Blackie knew me better than I knew myself. "I've got a couple of things I need to do this afternoon, but how about if I meet you at Pacific and Divisadero around seven thirty?"

"In front of Marks's house?" Blackie looked disgusted. "You're gonna die an early death, Ventana. I'll come by and pick you up here. We'll go in my car. If he's out, we're on."

"Does this mean you'll come?"

"Shit," he said. That meant yes.

After Blackie left, I went upstairs to call Rogelio Martinez. He wasn't at home, so he had to be at Spanish Heaven. I called him there and told him I'd be over in half an hour.

When I got there, the lunch crowd had cleared, and it was too early for dinner, at least for most. The place was empty, but Rogelio was back in the kitchen, hustling around, looking busy. He looked up and grinned handsomely when he saw me.

"Veronica," he said, and waved a ladle at me, "try these beans. I put extra cilantro and some *seranitos* in them. You tell me if they are too *bravo* for the *gringos.*"

I took a spoonful. It felt like I'd bitten into a firecracker. "Whoo! That's hot." I fanned my lips and he reached behind my back into the cooler.

"Try this," he said, snapping the lid off a Corona. I

grabbed it and chugged half the bottle in a couple of gulps.

"*Rico*, no?"

I set the beer down and grinned. "It's plenty *rico*, but don't serve it. You'll get yourself in trouble with the fire department."

He laughed. "Veronica, you have the mouth of a *gringo*. Your father, he did wrong. Not only did he refuse to teach you the language, he let you inherit your mother's *gringo* tongue. If you eat enough chiles, you will learn to love them."

"Keep telling me that," I said. "Maybe one day I'll believe you." After I finished the beer, I asked him about Murieta and Marks.

"Why do you ask me such things? I am no longer with those people."

"You used to be. I thought you might have heard something."

He shrugged. "If I had, I would have remembered. And if such a thing had happened, if Murieta had a connection with a famous judge like Judge Marks, believe me, *mi hija*, he would have bragged about it. It would have been news in the *barrio*. Murieta was not a modest man. He did not realize that the imagination of others could make him far grander than his own words ever could."

I tried to hide my disappointment. Rogelio put his hand over mine. "I am sorry, *mi hija*. These words, they are not what you wished to hear?"

"I guess not. Any chance they connected after you went straight?"

He shrugged. "That is possible."

"All right. I'll check it out, then." I reached for my purse. "Which brings me to—"

"Ah, no, no. I will not accept money from you today, *mi amor.* Your professional opinion of the beans was payment enough."

I put my billfold away and left just as the first dinner customers of the evening wandered in.

I spent the rest of the evening running errands—grocery shopping, cruising by Marks's house, cleaning the apartment, paying bills, and just killing time. When Blackie finally rolled around in his old Buick, I was ready.

But he didn't drive straight to Pacific Heights like I thought he would. We ended up out at Ocean Beach. I guessed he was looking for a place to talk. Since it was still light out, I didn't mind the wait. It was better to go in after dark anyway.

"So?" I asked, when he pulled into the lot overlooking the Sutro Baths and turned off the engine.

"I checked the place out."

"Good. So did I."

"You're a cagey doll, aren't you?"

"Learned from the best," I said, and winked at him. "I didn't see much from the street, but I thought the glass door on the east side looked good. Plenty of bushes, looked like a real flimsy lock, easy mark." Blackie nodded. He agreed. "I didn't see anything that looked like a security system, did you?"

"Don't sound so disappointed, doll. I know you like to bust alarms, but believe me, this way's easier." He put his big hands on his knees and pressed his back against the back of the seat. "You figured out yet what the fuck we're looking for?"

"I told you. Anything that'll tie Marks with either Murieta, since Noni said he worked for a judge sometimes, or with August, and thus Murieta."

"Like what?"

The sun dipped quietly behind the horizon before I answered. "I don't know," I said. "We'll just have to see what he's got for us."

It went like clockwork. Nobody was home, so we jimmied the lock on the glass door to the judge's study. It was just where we wanted to be.

The stuffy room reeked of stale cigar smoke, and the furnishings were dated but functional: bookshelves, a desk, chair, file cabinets, and a settee. A couple of imitation Monets broke the monotony of the dark wood paneling.

"Somebody ought to warn him he's living in a cracker box. A ten-year-old could break in here," I told Blackie. "This is really pitiful."

"Go ahead, you tell him. I ain't complainin'."

"But where's the challenge, Blackie?"

"Don't talk about challenge. You know what I say about challenge: Fuck it."

I took the desk and paused a minute to sense my parents' presence while Blackie sniffed around through the bookshelves and behind paintings. I was halfway through rifling the lap drawer when Blackie called out.

"Take a look at this." He sounded excited.

Blackie was over in the far corner. I crossed the room and he flicked his penlight upward against the wall. When he did, I saw what had charged him up: a wall safe.

"What do you say?" he asked, his voice full of enthusiasm. He rubbed his fingertips together. "*This* is more like it." Way back Blackie had taken safe-cracking lessons from an ex-con. Now he never saw a safe without working it over.

"If it will amuse you," I said, "go ahead."

I went back and finished the lap drawer, then worked the side ones. Staccato clicks snapped off the master dial while Blackie tinkered with the safe.

So far I'd gotten nowhere. Marks collected articles on birds, enjoyed reading hunting magazines, and kept a few copies of status reports from Greenside Convalescent. I scanned one, saw it was all a bunch of psychobabble about Mrs. Marks, and set it aside. Then from Blackie's side of the room I heard a quick, happy grunt.

"Aaah!"

"Did you get it?"

"Do dolphins swim?"

I closed the last drawer and crossed the room. Blackie was already pulling out what looked to be reams and reams of paper.

"What is all this?"

He handed me a stack. "Take a look."

I sank into a studded leather chair, set the pile on my lap, and flicked on my penlight. Flipping through the pages, I noticed each had the same format: a photograph in the upper right-hand corner, name, date of birth, and crimes synopsized on the left, and below, a text in narrative form. I'd seen them a zillion times before.

"These are parole reports, Blackie. What's Marks doing with these?"

"You got me."

"Think they're for his work?"

"You want to think that, go ahead. I say why keep 'em in his fucking safe?" Blackie leaned against the wall and leafed through a second stack of papers. "We got printouts here. Computer, looks like. He's underlined some of this shit."

I turned back to the pile of stuff on my lap. The pictures were all basically the same: young guys, Caucasian blonds, with light-colored eyes, either green or blue. There must have been a hundred and fifty reports. "I don't get it."

"This ain't normal for a judge," Blackie said. "Look at this shit. He's circled every line here that shows a conviction for rape. He's into some kind of cow shit."

"Are the names on those printouts in any kind of order? Alpha or chronological?"

He knew what I wanted right away. "Alpha," he said. "Murieta's not on here."

"Wilson?"

He paged to the back. "No. . . . Gummy neither. Give me a name off one of those reports." I did, and he rustled through the pages. "Here it is, circled big as you please."

"Let me see that."

He brought the packet over and pointed.

"Try this one." I read him another and he found it, circled, too. "You know what he's doing?" I said incredulously. "He's using these police printouts to find rapists who've been paroled."

"What the hell for? Revenge?"

I shook my head. "I wish I knew."

"Whatever it is, the old man's made a science out of it. He must be nuts."

I stood up and eyed a file cabinet against the wall. "Do me a favor, Blackie." I reached over to the desk for a pen and some paper and handed them to him. "Write down as many of these guys as you can. I'm going to take a look at those files over there."

I shouldn't have wasted my time. The cabinet drawers were worthless. They were filled with a bunch of receipts and income tax returns. Big deal. I slid the last drawer shut and stood up.

"Let's get out of here. I'm getting antsy. We've been here too long."

Blackie stacked the reports back in the safe and snapped the door shut. "Let's get the hell out of Dodge," he said.

Back in the car Blackie said, "I got a feeling we ain't got squat. What's so illegal about a fucking judge having police reports in his house?"

"I don't know, Blackie. But don't write it all off yet. Maybe I can come up with a new theory."

"Yeah? Like what?"

"I don't know. I'll have to think about it, see what makes sense. Drop me off at the apartment, okay?"

"Joey's playing at the—"

"Thanks, Blackie, but I'll pass. I need to think."

"Hey, doll, you're getting too fucking serious about this. Remember, there ain't no paycheck in it for you."

31

The phone answering machine's indicator light blinked at me when I walked in the door. There was only one call. It was from Sarah Scopes, the Coast Guard captain's wife.

"I have something for you," she said when I played the message back. "Some information. Please call me tonight if you can before ten. Otherwise I'll have to ask you to call me in the morning."

I checked my watch. Damn! It was a quarter after. I'd have to wait. When I dialed Post to see if he'd turned up anything since we last talked, I found out he wasn't in and wasn't expected until Monday. I needed to think, but that didn't mean I had to sit around all night. It was too early to go to sleep and too late to catch a movie. I didn't feel like drinking, but my juices were still bubbling from the Marks break-in.

After brewing a pot of coffee I dumped it in a Thermos and headed out the door. If nothing else, I could keep an eye on August. It'd give me time to think and make me feel constructive at the same time. He was probably at home by now, and if he wasn't, well, I could have a look around inside.

The Marin County district where August lived was steeped in wealth and eucalyptus trees. Nobody built a house there unless they could do it on a cliff or a hillside and nothing was under three—most were four—stories high, redwood, with the driveway and garage on the roof and the rest of the house underneath it and out of sight. A couple of places along the drive up Mount Tam were level with the road, but mostly all you could see were a bunch of locked-up garages and mailboxes.

August's place was 27 Hillside. Too appropriate, I thought, as I wound Mitch's Citroën up to the top, then started back down again. Just over the crest a single mailbox stuck out from a stand of bushes. It said "27." That had to be it.

I eased the car to the side of the road and shut off the lights and engine, then stared at the lot until my eyes got used to the dark. August's house was like all the others, out of sight from the road, deep in the trees. Behind all the shrubbery, all I could make out was a black BMW and a motorcycle parked in the carport. The motorcycle could be his. Or it could mean he had company.

The place was definitely a new challenge in surveillance. I parked the car across the street and down the road a little bit, then walked back up and poked around the low-hanging eucalyptus branches. There were some narrow wooden slat steps leading down into the dark and tons of stinking, rotten wet foliage all over the place.

I tiptoed down the stairs and peeked into the first lighted window I saw. It was a bedroom—the master bedroom—and somebody was in it.

August wasn't alone. There was a woman with him, and he didn't have any clothes on, but then neither did she. Unless her leather harness, black garter belt, and black stockings counted. And what they were doing looked like something off of Lon Wilson's TV set. August was splayed across the bed on his stomach, alone, and his huge body was one pulsing, sweaty mess. Whatever was going on, it was really pulling his strings.

I looked to see what his partner was doing. Her back was to me so I couldn't see her face, but her straight, dark hair cascaded off her shoulders when she leaned over to tie August's wrists and ankles to the bedposts. When she picked up a short leather whip and I realized I was still watching them, I turned away, disgusted with myself and a little ashamed to be doing what I was doing.

Now what? It looked like they were set for the night. There was no point in watching, no point in staying. I didn't want to stick around, but I wasn't totally convinced I should go.

Through the glass I heard the snap of the whip and then moans. I wondered what Philly Post would say if I told him what was going on. Big, macho Pete August, the "real P.I.," tied to his own bed, getting a whipping. His groans filtered out, unnerving me until it dawned on me that he wasn't hurting. The sounds he was making were sounds of ecstasy. I shuddered. This had to be ten times more sleazy than divorce surveillance, no question.

After one last peek I stood up to go, but something that wasn't there before pressed against my leg. I looked down and gasped, jumped away and lost my balance, then fell right on top of a cat. It yowled loud enough to wake the dead, then skittered off into the bushes.

"Shit!" I scrambled to my feet in time to see August's girlfriend face the window. I took one look at her and froze. It was Martha Coyle. *Judge* Martha Coyle.

It was stupid, but all I could think was that the judge

was passing a very private sentence on a very private private investigator. I started to giggle, lost my balance again, and tumbled down a couple of steps, then picked myself up a second time and looked inside.

Judge Coyle's lips were moving, and I could hear her voice but couldn't make out what she was saying. August was squirming facedown on the bed, but *his* voice was coming in loud and clear.

"Untie me! Untie me!"

When Judge Coyle started on his left ankle, I turned and shot up the steps, two at a time. Just as I reached the top one, I heard something behind me—a soft, shuffling noise. It couldn't be him. But when I looked over my shoulder, it was.

He was wearing a pair of gym shorts, no shirt, and his breath came out in big white puffs as he panted after me. I couldn't help but think that if he'd taken the time to put on a shirt, I'd have had a better chance to get away.

When he caught up with me, he grabbed my ankle and hung on in the dark, winded and furious. I wrangled to get my foot loose, but his fingers held on like iron calipers. He dragged me toward him, bumping me down a couple of steps.

"What are you doing here?" he shouted.

"My cat," I said, and hoped he couldn't see my face. I could hardly make his out. "I was looking for my cat."

"The hell you were." He was breathless from the run up the steps, or maybe it was from the cold. I hoped it was from the run, because what I planned to do next depended on him being out of breath.

He was two steps below me, just far away enough for me to raise my free leg and punch him in the chest with it. And that's exactly what I did.

He let go of my foot to grab for the banister, and I

kicked him again, harder this time, with both heels. He teetered. When he lost his balance and tumbled away, down into the darkness, I scrambled to my feet and ran like hell.

I raced down the road to the car, started the engine, and coasted out of sight with the headlights off. I didn't turn them on until I was a good quarter of a mile down the road. Then I sped down the mountain to the city as fast as lightning, checking the rearview mirror every five minutes to make sure he wasn't behind me.

After I crossed the bridge, I made a wide loop through town just in case. A few quick turns and narrow passes, then I headed home to North Beach.

I didn't feel safe until I got upstairs and unlocked the door. But as soon as I stepped inside, I knew something was wrong. A vague, sweet scent, something I'd never smelled before, made the tiny hairs on the back of my neck stand on end. I reached for the light and turned it on, then just about fainted. There, sitting on the sofa bed like he'd been sitting there waiting for me all night, was Pete August.

32

I decided my best shot at survival was to sound indignant. "What do you want?" I demanded.

"That's what I'd like to know. What were you doing at my house?"

"I—"

"Why don't you come in and sit down?"

I hesitated. August was big and strong and he owed me one for shoving him down the stairs. I'd already seen him throttle one man and I knew he wouldn't have any qualms about thumping me. I stayed put.

"How'd you get in?"

"Trade secret," he said. "You should have learned it by now if you're a detective."

He sounded all right—more annoyed than angry. He didn't look stupid, or crazy-mad either. I'd probably be okay so long as I didn't get too far from the door. I pulled my keys out of the lock and closed the door, then leaned against the wall.

"Don't you want to sit?" he asked.

"What do you want?"

"Why are you trying to pin Murieta's murder on me?"

"I'm just trying to prove you were where you say you weren't."

"Is someone paying you to do this?"

"Of course not."

"What if I told you I was there?"

"I'd say, 'Tell the cops.'"

"They aren't asking."

"They did. You told them you were at your office."

"When my friends told me what you were implying, I had no choice. You don't expect me to hang myself?"

"But you admit you were there?"

He fixed me with a smooth smile. Up close, his boxy features were attractive. "Just between the two of us," he said.

"All right. You admit you were there. That pretty much narrows it down."

"I talked to Murieta. I roughed him up. But I didn't kill him."

"You threw him in the Bay."

"I did. But he was alive when he went in. The coroner's report states explicitly that he was killed *first, then* put in the water."

I stared at his face and wondered why such a nice, normal-looking man would want his girlfriend to tie him up and work him over. Maybe his folks didn't spank him enough when he was a kid. Or maybe they spanked him too much. I kept picturing the guy naked and squirming like I'd seen him less than an hour ago, and I felt myself blush.

"How do you know about the autopsy?" I said, trying to cover in case he'd followed my thoughts. I hadn't seen the report, and Philly Post hadn't mentioned it either.

He tilted his head and smiled at me. "Friends. Don't you have friends?"

"Oh, you mean like Officer Ryan?"

"Pat Ryan is one of many." He leaned back against the couch and spread his arms along the back on either side of him. He acted like he owned the place. "Listen, Miss Ventana, no one's going to believe you. The evidence isn't strong enough, and do you know why? Do you know why your little setup, if that's what it is, won't work?"

He was talking calm and easy. Even if the words he picked were tough, he didn't sound like a bully. In spite of myself I listened.

"It won't work because I didn't do it. He was alive when he went in."

We stared at each other for a while. I was wondering what he was thinking and I guess he was doing the same. I said, "You want me to drop the whole thing."

"It will never stand up in court, if you ever get it there. It would save you a lot of trouble to just forget it."

"And you too."

He shrugged, but didn't say anything.

"All right," I said. "Suppose you didn't kill him. What were you doing there? Why'd you beat him up?"

"If I tell you, will you forget the whole thing? Will you forget what you saw tonight?" The dark shading of his five-o'clock shadow deepened. I wasn't the only one who was blushing.

"What you do behind closed doors is your business. I apologize. But maybe next time, you know, you ought to think about pulling the shades or something."

"I think I'll do that," he said, and I knew right then and there I was out of the woods. He wasn't going to manhandle me or beat me up. I felt so relieved, all I could think about was how thirsty I was.

"How about a beer?" I crossed the room over to the fridge. "Anchor Steam all right?" He said no, so I pulled one out for myself and sat down at the table across from him. I was still closer to the door than he was.

"I don't expect you to repeat what I'm going to tell you," he said. "If you do, I'll deny ever being here. You have nothing that can prove otherwise, and I have an alibi."

"Back at your house?"

He nodded.

"Okay, what's the story?"

"Murieta threatened me on several occasions—"

"With what?"

"That's immaterial. What *is* important is that his threats were escalating, and although I usually take no notice of his type, I felt, upon this instance, that strong action was needed to dissuade him from further harassment."

"So you meet him down at Fort Point Monday morning and throttle him?"

"In essence, yes. I wanted to frighten him and I accomplished that. But I didn't kill him."

I set the beer down on the table and crossed my arms. "Is that it? Is that all you're going to say, 'cause if it is, I—"

"It's the truth. What more can you want?"

"How about the nature of his threats? Why did you take him seriously when you don't anybody else?"

"Those particulars are immaterial."

"Maybe to you, Mr. August, but I need to know."

He leveled his eyes on me. "Why?"

"Because with justification I might believe you. Right now I get the feeling you've got something to hide. Does this have anything to do with Judge Marks . . . or your sister?"

Surprise flickered on his face, then anger. He stood up, and my legs tensed. I was ready to hit the door, but he stood right where he was.

"I feel no compunction to bare my personal life to you any further, Miss Ventana. You may choose to believe me or you may not. In any event I expect you to cease and desist your prowling about my home, my office, and my life. Leave me and my family alone. If you persist in this harassment, I'll speak to my attorney. I'll make very sure you never work in this city again. Good night."

I waited a civilized few seconds after he closed the door, then sprinted down the stairs after him. But he was gone; he'd disappeared. The black BMW was nowhere in sight. I went into the Quarter Moon and stopped at the first table by the window. Three long-hairs were splitting a tall bottle of Jim Beam and playing liar's dice.

"Did you see a man walk by outside? About six feet tall, thick black hair and a shock of white at the temple?"

They looked at me like I was speaking Latin, so I skipped them and went on to the next table. They understood, but they just shook their heads. I asked at the next table, and the next. Nobody had seen a thing.

"Damn!" I trudged upstairs and finished my beer in a snit. He actually had me over a barrel. Sure, there was a body and sure, he'd been there, but he'd never admit it and nobody'd believe me over him. Nobody had so far. It came down to August's word against mine, and between his connections in the community and the D.A.'s office, he'd never get put away. No wonder he was so civilized. He could afford to be.

33

"**T**ell the lady what you saw, Johnny," Sarah Scopes said.

We were, all four of us—me, Johnny, and John and Sarah Scopes—sitting around the kitchen table at the Coast Guard house. The kid had his bright red binoculars around his neck and he sat in his chair like there was a harsh, bare bulb over his head and five armed guards ready to beat the information out of him.

"Tell her, son," the captain urged.

The kid looked up, caught my eye, and quickly looked back down at the table. His eyes were watering. Not a witness who inspired confidence, by any means.

"He's afraid because he wasn't supposed to be up there," Sarah explained. Then to Johnny. "It's all right, Johnny. I promise, you won't get a spanking unless you do it again. Just tell the lady what you told me, okay?"

I wondered what little Johnny thought about his parents and me, all hovering over him, hanging on his every twitch.

"Come on, Johnny," his mother said.

He fidgeted and scraped at something real or imagined on the table's slick, polished surface.

"I was camping," he began, eyes down, voice barely audible.

"I remember that," I said. I tried to sound soft and encouraging, like Sarah, but I didn't know if I was pulling it off or not. I didn't have much experience with kids. "You had a tent in the yard." I pointed out the back door. "Out there."

Johnny nodded without looking up. He was totally absorbed in scraping whatever it was off the table. He was probably past the first layer of varnish by now, but Sarah Scopes didn't seem to mind.

"I snuck out of the tent," Johnny mumbled, "and went up in the bushes with Mac."

"Our dog," Sarah explained. "What did you see from up there? Tell Ronnie what you saw."

"A man."

I held my breath. "What man, Johnny? What did he look like?" He finally looked up and his eyes met mine. I smiled at him. This time he didn't look away.

"The man who threw the other man in the water."

"What did he look like?" I was afraid I'd spook him if I pressed him too hard.

"Tell her how you saw them," Sarah prompted.

The ghost of a smile appeared on his face, and he touched the red binoculars on his chest. "My binoclars," he said, mispronouncing the word. "I looked at him like that." He raised them to his face and looked through them at me.

"I see," I said.

"Tell her what he looked like," John Scopes urged.

"He looked funny, like a skunk."

The streak of white in August's hair. That was one way of describing him.

"Should we be taping this or something?" Sarah asked.

I shook my head and kept my eyes on the kid. "What color was his hair, Johnny? Do you remember?"

"Black."

"What was he wearing? Did you get a look at his clothes?"

"A suit like my Grandpa wears."

"And the other man? You said there were two of them. What was the other man wearing?"

"Blue. Brown."

"A blue jacket?"

He nodded.

"Tan pants?"

His head bobbed again.

"What did they do?"

The boy's face clouded over. "They had a fight. The skunk man won. He hurt the little man. I thought he was dead." The boy looked across the table at me.

"What made you think that?"

"The skunk man threw the other man in the water. He didn't come out for a real long time, so I thought he was drownded."

"WHAT!" I shouted. The kid just about jumped out of his skin. I guess I overreacted. I sat back down again, took a deep breath, and told myself to relax. "I'm sorry, Johnny. I'm sorry if I scared you. But what you're saying is important to me. It's real important." He looked up. He was listening. "You saw the blue and tan man come *out of the water?*"

He nodded.

"Where?"

"He came out at the rocks."

"Was he walking?"

Johnny nodded again. *Damn!*

"Where did he go?"

"Up the hill. You know the stairs—"

"Yes," I said. "The ones up to the parking lot on the hill?"

"Yeah."

Double damn! August hadn't lied. Before, I had a murderer and no body. Now I had a body, or rather three, and no murderer. I forced a smile.

"I'm glad we talked, Johnny. Do you think you can tell the police what you've told me? If your mom or your dad go with you?"

He looked from one to the other, then nodded.

"Good. You're a real brave boy." I stood and so did John and Sarah. They walked me to the door, and once we were outside, I said, "Thanks for calling me first. I hope you don't mind talking to the police. They'll have to know."

John Scopes said, "Well . . . we knew that." He caught his wife's eye and she smiled sheepishly. "Sarah talked me into calling you first. She said you'd be gentle with him and should get first crack."

"Was I?" I asked.

"Like his own mother," Sarah said. She took my hand and squeezed it. "Thanks. I'm worried about what it'll be like with the police, though."

"Don't be. They've got special officers to deal with kids." Of which I was certain Philly Post was not. "They know what to say and what not to say so they won't frighten or bias them."

"I'd like to wait a day before talking to them. This morning was kind of rough on him."

I hesitated. Post would accuse me of withholding evidence. But no way around it, he was going to be angry no matter what I did. What difference would a day make? "I'm sure Lieutenant Post would understand," I lied.

"Will you come with us?" Sarah asked. Her husband didn't say anything, but he nodded when I glanced over at him.

"Sure, I'll be glad to." I didn't have the heart to tell them that where Philly Post was concerned, they'd probably be better off without me.

34

It was a good thing they waited a day. Philly Post really would have been pissed if I'd called him in on a Sunday. As it was, he held himself in check until after the Scopeses were gone and the two of us were back in his office alone. Then he plodded to his desk, collapsed in his chair, and covered his face with his hands. I closed the door and sat across from him.

"I'm sorry," I said.

His hands dropped away from his face. *"You're* sorry. *I'm* out of a promotion. Where was this kid before? What took him so long to talk about it?"

"His mother said he was scared. It's a shock for a child to see something like that. Christ, he's only eight years old. It was a shock for *me.*"

"At least *he* kept his head and didn't go off half-cocked shouting 'murder.' "

"Look, I said I was sorry."

"Yeah, yeah. Okay, that's it." He stood up. "Case closed. We'll wrap it up."

I didn't move. "What about the bodies?"

"What about them?"

"Somebody had to kill all those people."

"You know what, Ventana? You're absolutely right. But I'm going to tell you something: It's none of your damned business. I want you to stay out of it, understand?"

I gave him my best I-know-you-don't-really-mean-that smile. "Hey, I thought we were partners."

"You got that right. *Were.* Come on, get moving. You're taking up space in here."

I pushed myself out of the chair. "What about . . . ?"

He shook his head and I sighed.

"Will you at least throw me a bone every once in a while? I mean, if I were to call you . . . ?"

"Not on your life. Now, butt out. You're lucky to get out of here alive after what you've done to my career."

"Hey, it can't be that bad. And if it is, I heard good cops make great P.I.'s."

It wasn't exactly a smile, but it was as close to one as he'd come that afternoon. I winked. "Keep in touch."

35

"**H**e and Martha Coyle? Shit. I thought she had more class than that."

"Now, Blackie. I didn't tell you so you could pass judgment. You're sworn to secrecy."

"What difference does it make now? August's off the hook."

"Sure. But somebody murdered Jake Murieta. And Lon Wilson. And Purdue."

"Don't tell me you're still working with Post on this."

"Not exactly."

"He threw you out of his office, didn't he?"

I picked up the styrofoam box my hamburger had come in and tossed my napkin and empty mustard package into it. I didn't answer because I didn't want to.

Blackie looked triumphant. "I told you cops are shit. You can't trust the fuckers."

"Oh, Post's not so bad."

"Ventana, he tossed you on your can, didn't he?"

"Sort of. I think he kinda felt obligated to."

"Don't kid yourself, doll. Cops'll crap in your face just for the fun of it."

I sat down on Blackie's lumpy couch and looked out at the vacant farmers' market down the slope from his house. It was Monday. Had it been Saturday, every farmer from the Central Valley would have been there hawking his harvest. I stuffed my litter into a bag. "You know, I've been thinking, Blackie."

"You come up with a theory on why Maximum Marks has got that shit in his safe?"

"No."

"Did you ask Post about it?"

"Uh-uh."

Blackie chuckled. "See, you don't trust the fucker either."

"All right, maybe I don't, but I'm just being careful, that's all. I think I ought to go see Noni again. You know, Jake Murieta's mistress."

"Why?"

"Maybe she forgot something. Maybe I did. She's got to be in better shape than when I saw her the first time."

"You're not making any money on this, doll."

"I know. But that missing-person case paid enough to last me three months. It's only been two and a half weeks. Besides, nobody's beating a path to my door with a paying case."

Blackie crumpled the wrapper in his hand and dug into the bag for a second sandwich. "This shit's under your skin, isn't it?"

"What? The case?"

"Fuck the case. I mean the fucking business."

36

Noni was behind the counter between a colorful Dior display and a three-foot-high cardboard cutout of a new perfume called Poison. She looked ten times more chic than she had the other day, and I wondered how long it took her to put on her makeup. I'd heard somewhere that the more natural a woman looked, the longer it took, and Noni looked so fresh and glowing, I guessed it must have taken her a day or two.

She seemed to recognize me, but the expression on her face betrayed that she couldn't quite place me. I was sure she wouldn't have looked so friendly if she'd remembered the last time we met. I smiled back.

"Hi."

The sound of my voice seemed to jar her into partial recall. She wrinkled her delicate, arched brows in a pretty imitation of a woman thinking.

"I'm sorry, I don't—"

"Ronnie Ventana," I said. "We talked the other day."

Her face went white, and suddenly the makeup was vividly apparent, like a mask. Her smile dissolved.

"I'm sorry to bother you here," I said, "but I need to talk to you again."

"About Jake?"

"Yeah."

Noni glanced significantly at the customers milling around the cosmetics counter. There were a bunch of them: blue-haired old ladies with parchment for skin, some foreign-looking women, and a couple of drop-dead blondes in leather dresses.

"It doesn't have to be here," I told her. "We can talk anywhere you want. Don't you get a break or something?"

"I'm scheduled for one twenty minutes from now. Can you wait?"

"Sure. How about across the street in the park?"

I found a bench and spent the next twenty minutes counting the bums and the pigeons in Union Square. The pigeons outnumbered the street people five to one, no contest. Otherwise the park was a nice place to sit and soak up the sun. It was relatively clean, with the emphasis on *relatively,* and quiet.

I closed my eyes and tilted my head back to get the full strength of the rays on my face. It felt good. I must have dozed, because all of a sudden my face went cold. A shadow crossed between me and the sun, and it took me a minute to remember where I was. I opened one eye and saw Noni's thin silhouette outlined against the sky.

"The sun's bad for your skin," she said, and sat down next to me. "Are you wearing a sun block?"

I dropped my hand and stared at Noni Witherspoon. She looked just as perfect and delicate in natural light as she did inside the store. Amazing. I shook my head in wonder, and Noni took it for an answer.

"It's so important," she assured me. "The sun ages a

woman. Come back to the store with me after my break and I'll give you a sample."

"Thanks." I sat up. "About Mr. Murieta . . ."

"Did you find the killer?"

"It turns out I didn't see him killed. Did you know Pete August was a suspect?"

"Is that why you asked me about him?" I nodded and she looked away. "Do you think he did it?"

"No. Another witness cleared him."

"But you said you saw—"

"The witness is an eight-year-old boy. I talked to him yesterday before the cops did.. August roughed Mr. Murieta up, he even threw him in the Bay, but the shock of the cold water must have brought him around." I shrugged. "I'm no doctor, but it must have been something like that. You said he was a strong swimmer. Anyway, the boy saw him walk away from the water later, I guess after I was gone."

Noni puckered up her forehead and seemed to take it all in. She looked like a sad little princess with a broken dream.

"Who did it, then?" she finally asked.

I shrugged again.

Her beautiful eyes studied me mournfully. "Are you still trying to find out?"

"Officially no." Then, "You said before that Jake did some work for a judge."

"That's right. She lives in Pacific Heights."

I sat up. "What? What did you say? Did you say '*she*'?"

She blinked. "Jake always said 'she.' "

"How do you know where she lives?" I guess I was shouting. One of the bag ladies turned around and stared.

"Jake mentioned it once. I always paid attention when

he talked about other women." *What about when he talked about his wife?* I wondered. "You seem surprised," Noni said serenely. "Didn't I tell you the last time we talked?"

"No."

"I'm sorry. I was so upset that day, I'm not sure what I said."

"Did he ever mention the name Martha Coyle to you?" It was a long shot, but she was the only female judge I knew and she had been in August's bedroom. But Noni shook her head. Pale wisps of hair fell across her forehead.

"I don't think so. I really can't remember."

"You said he would find people. Did he do that for this judge?"

"I don't know. He never said he was a private detective; that's what I called him. He told me sometimes he was more like an enforcer and a boss rolled into one."

"What did he mean by that?"

"I don't know. I guess that he was pretty important."

I watched two pigeons face off, each puffing up his feathers to look twice his size. If both were doing the same thing to intimidate the other, how could it possibly work? I wondered. While they strutted and postured, a little sparrow snuck in and grabbed the crumb they were fighting over. I looked back at the beautiful woman beside me.

"Did he work for that judge often?"

"I don't know. He really didn't say much about his work."

"Did he ever work with other people? Do you know anybody who could help me out? Any friends or associates of his?"

She started to shake her head, hesitated, then frowned.

"He liked to work alone. He said it was simpler that way." She looked at her watch and stood up. "I have to go back inside. It's so depressing to talk about Jake like this." She closed her eyes, then opened them. "Do I look all right? Do I look depressed?"

"You look fine," I said, and got up too. "One more thing. Do you have a picture of him?"

"Of course." She fumbled through her purse and pulled out a snapshot. "This was our anniversary," she said, handing it to me with a wistful smile. I looked at it. She was in a formal gown and he was wearing a tux. Jake didn't look at all like the lump they'd hauled out of the Bay the other night.

"Can I keep it?"

"As long as you give it back."

"No problem."

Noni started up the walk, then stopped. "Your sunscreen."

I shrugged, followed her inside, and accepted the two-ounce bottle of vitamin E hydrolyzed sun block. Now I could face the sun and not be afraid.

37

Martha Coyle wasn't listed in the phone book. That meant I'd have to wait for the state bar association to open in the morning to get the address from them. In the meantime I decided it might be worthwhile to talk to Murieta's wife. Sometimes people had a lot more to say when they knew there was no chance of retribution.

Three blocks from Murieta's house I spotted his niece walking with another girl and three sleazy-looking toughs. The boys looked about eighteen. Too old for her, I thought as I pulled over and honked. The boys looked at me like I was crazy and the girl didn't recognize me at first, but then she smiled, said something to the group, and walked over to the car.

I rolled down the passenger-side window. "Hi, remember me?"

She stuck her head inside and rested her arms against the door. Her eyes still had that odd, haunted quality, but the rest of her looked like any fifteen-year-old girl trying to look and act eighteen. "You're the lady P.I. Are you still trying to find out who killed Uncle Jake?"

"Uh-huh."

"Nice car. Is this real leather?" She reached in and stroked the backrest.

"Yeah."

"Yours?"

"Actually it's my ex's. We switched cars for a couple of days."

"You got any cigarettes?"

"I don't smoke."

"Any beer?"

"In my fridge at home," I said, and smiled. She was making me remember how tough it was to be fifteen. "I was on my way over to see your aunt. Need a ride home?"

"Nope. I just came out." She opened the car door and got in anyway. "You can talk to me."

"I already have." I eyed the junior thugs on the corner. "What about your friends?"

She glanced out the window. Her buddies were in a sullen circle in front of a metal-grated storefront, looking bored. But then they'd looked bored when I drove up.

"They're not my friends. They're from the neighborhood and said they were coming out, so I said I'd come too."

"What's your name?"

"Marina."

"How old are those boys, Marina? Do you go to school with them?"

Marina looked amused. "You think they're too old for me, don't you?"

"They seem a lot older than you. Are they?"

"I don't know." She sighed and looked at me. "Are you *Chicana*?"

"My father was Mexican."

Marina grinned. "I thought so. How'd you become a P.I.? Was that what your father was?"

"He and my mom died when I was about your age. They were cat burglars."

The kid's eyes just about popped out of her head. "No," she said in disbelief. "Did they teach you anything, like how to break into places and stuff?"

"They didn't think that would be a good idea."

She still didn't believe me. "I bet they did. You're not really a P.I. It's a cover, huh?"

"I don't need a cover. I really am a private investigator." I glanced at the group on the sidewalk. "Listen, are you sure you don't want a ride home?"

"Uh-huh," she said, but she didn't move. "I guess you want to ask my aunt about Uncle Jake."

"Right."

"Why don't you just talk to me?"

"We already talked, Marina. You told me Jake was into physical abuse and that he had a girlfriend. Is there anything else you think I should know?"

"He was a bastard. I hated him."

"Do you know anything about what kind of work he did?"

"The hits? Yeah. I thought everybody knew that." She said it matter-of-factly, like everybody's uncle killed for a living. "He was strictly Little League. He tried to get in with the *Nuestra Familia,* but they wouldn't take him. He was too big a jerk even for them."

"Did he talk to you about it?"

She snickered. "Hardly."

"But you knew?"

"Sure. Look, this stuff is what you call common knowledge. Even the kids at school know about him. My aunt knows, too, but God, she's warped. She swears it's all lies." She pulled out a stick of gum, unwrapped it, folded it in thirds, then stuck it in her mouth.

"Did he ever mention a judge? A woman judge?"

The girl giggled. "I didn't know there was such a thing." She snapped her gum and shrugged. "He didn't really talk to us. He told my aunt he sold shoes. Can you imagine *him* selling shoes?"

I pictured the swollen purple lump washed up on the rocks off Pier 45. "No."

"Me neither." Marina laughed and for the first time looked like the young girl she was: vulnerable, naked without bravado. "Didn't they arrest somebody?" she asked after a minute.

"Not yet."

"Too bad. I want to call him up when they do and thank him for the favor. Whoever did it deserves a medal." She snapped her gum again, looking straight ahead. "I used to watch him, you know, follow him around and just watch. He always thought I was doing something else, but no, man, I was watching him. I knew if I did it long enough, I'd find something out, something I could tell the cops, so they'd put him away. Maybe forever." The fire of hate burned in her eyes. Then the light in them faded. "Do you think I'm bad?"

"No," I said, and I didn't even have to think about it. "You're just human, that's all. It's natural to dislike somebody who's mean to you." I couldn't tell what she thought about my answer because she didn't say anything for a while. Finally I said, "Is that how you found out about Noni Witherspoon? By following him?"

"Yeah. Did you go talk to her?"

I nodded. "That's how I found out about the judge. Did you ever follow him to Pacific Heights?"

"Sure." She grinned when she realized I was interested. "There's a big rock house there. Joe, my friend—"

I glanced over to the group on the corner, and Marina followed my gaze.

"No, not them," she said. "Joe's closer to my age, but he's got his license. I talked Joe into following Uncle Jake one day, and that's where he went. It was a big house. He never got inside, though. They just answered the door and sent him away."

"Do you think you could show me where?"

Marina shook her head. "I get all turned around off my turf. I don't even remember what street it was."

"If you saw it—if I showed you the house—would you recognize it?"

"I guess." She didn't sound too convinced.

"Good. Want to go for a ride?"

"Sure."

We drove over to Judge Marks's house, but when I pointed it out, Marina swore it wasn't the place. She thought it was nearby, but wasn't exactly sure where. By the time we got back to the Mission district, the group Marina had come out with had drifted and spread out onto the sidewalk.

"Listen," I said. "Are you sure I can't give you a ride home?"

"No thanks." Marina opened the door and got out. I watched her join the group as they oozed across the street like some giant amoeba. Kids.

When I got to Murieta's house, nobody was home. It was just as well. After all, I didn't know how much Mrs. Murieta could help if she thought her husband was a shoe salesman. I picked up a pizza on the way home, filled the tub, and had dinner there while I read yesterday's Sunday *New York Times*.

38

By the time I finished my run the next morning, had breakfast, and drove to three different offices downtown to deliver Tuxedo Messages, it was close to one o'clock. I grabbed a piroshki at a little place on Montgomery Street, then, still wearing my tux, drove down to the state bar association to get Martha Coyle's address. While I was there, I picked up a bio sheet on her too.

As soon as I got back in my car, I unfolded the sheet to read it. A yellow Maserati pulled up next to me, and the blond hunk of sun-tanned muscle inside raised his eyebrows at me. In any other town I would have been flattered, but this was San Francisco, and I knew he wasn't after my body; he just wanted my parking place.

I shook my head and waved him on, then looked at the bio sheet again. Martha Coyle's address was listed. So were the dates and particulars of her graduation from college and law school, admission to the bar, all the jobs she'd held, and the date she was appointed to the bench. At the very bottom of the page was a statement attesting to the fact that no complaints against her had been found valid by the association.

I folded the sheet, tucked it into my purse, then changed my clothes at home and drove to Marina's house to wait for her to come home from school. While I waited, I talked to Mrs. Murieta. Marina was right about her aunt. The old lady told me absolutely nothing of value and broke down in tears every five minutes. Old crying-jag Noni was better than her. She was totally worthless as a witness. When Marina finally showed up, I was so happy to see her, I wanted to hug her. Instead I just got us out of there as fast as I could.

"What'd I tell you?" Marina said as soon as we were out the door. "Isn't she a weirdo?"

I didn't agree, out of respect for my elders, but I didn't disagree either. Marina let it go and on the drive over to Pacific Heights told me all about a senior she had a crush on. She asked me how to get a date with him.

"Why don't you just ask him out?" I suggested.

"What? Are you kidding?"

"This *is* the nineties, you know."

"What if he says no? I'll die."

"Just concentrate on somebody else, then. If you're anything like I was in high school, you'll fall crazy in love with somebody else in a week."

"Yeah?"

"Sure. Trust me."

"I don't know. I think maybe I'll ask him, but if he says no, I'm just going to die."

I pulled over mid-block on Vallejo Street, just around the corner from Scott. The neighborhood had class. Old money lived here: tidy little green lawns, Mercedes and Cadillacs, and everything done out in understated elegance, quiet and well tended. Every house was a mansion. I pointed to 2640.

"Is that it?"

The house on the other side of the street and down was a two-story stone structure with winding steps leading up to the front door. On the first level and to the side was an attached garage. Little round shrubs surrounded the house and lined the walkway. There was a huge cypress in the middle of the yard.

Marina leaned across me to see out the windshield.

"Yeah! That's it!" She looked at me with amazement. "How did you find it?"

"A hunch. You said he never went inside?"

"Uh-uh. He went up there, and they made him wait outside. Then he talked to somebody and went back to his car. I didn't think it was any big deal. Is it?" Her dark eyes weren't sullen anymore. They were dancing with curiosity. I had to smile.

"It might be. I need to check things out some more."

"Aren't you going to go up there? Aren't you going to see who lives there?"

"I know who lives there," I said. "And before I do anything, I'm taking you home."

"Aaawww. Pleeeaase. I bet I can help."

"Not the way you're thinking. You've helped me loads, already, Marina. I appreciate it but—"

"Let me hang out with you. We can go talk to whoever lives there and ask them what Uncle Jake wanted."

I turned the engine over and pulled out. "Not a chance. If you want to do P.I. work, you've got to have a license. And to get a license, you've got to get a few years on you first. How old are you?"

"I'll be fifteen in September."

"That's what I thought. You're way too young."

"But I—"

"Listen. I'll make a deal with you. Look me up when you finish school. High school. I promise I'll teach you whatever I know."

"But . . . two whole years away? I could be dead by then."

"That's as good as it gets, kid. Deal or no deal?"

Marina shoved her bottom lip out in a pout, but I think she was doing it more out of obligation than anger. No matter how loud she howled, I knew she was excited about getting a ticket out of the Mission. It was probably the first legal offer she'd had.

"Okay," she said when she finally figured out her carping wasn't doing the job. "I guess."

I dropped her off at Dolores Park, then drove back to Martha Coyle's house. I rang the buzzer and heard the chimes inside. While I waited, the discreet Riley Security logo in the corner of the window nearest me caught my eye.

Riley was supposed to be the best security firm in town, and a logo like that meant only one thing to me: It was a challenge to get inside. I made a mental note to try it after I wrapped this case up. It'd be a good exercise, sort of like continuing education. Maybe Blackie would want to come along too.

I hung around Judge Coyle's door for about five minutes and rang the bell some more, but nobody answered, so I assumed Her Honor was out. Probably still at work. It looked like Judge Coyle didn't believe in hired help. Either that, or it was the butler's day off. My fingers itched for the burglar alarm pad next to the door, but I'd left my stuff out in the car, and if I went back for it now, I'd look too suspicious.

I gave up and was almost back to the Citroën when I

saw a woman in a pink-and-white uniform carrying a yellow bag pop out of the house next door and head for a blue Mercedes in the driveway. I crossed the lawn and caught up with her just as she started the engine. She switched it off when I came up to her, rolled her window down, and said with a smile, "Can I help you, honey?"

"I hope so," I said. "I was just next door, but I don't think there's anybody home. Doesn't Judge Coyle have a housekeeper?"

"She used to. Hilda Gutierrez. But Hilda quit two months ago. She uses Tidy Homes now. They're a service."

"Actually," I said, "it's Mrs. Gutierrez I'm looking for. How could I get hold of her?"

"Hilda?" She tilted her head back and looked at me. "Is she in trouble of some kind?"

"Not really. It's a long story." I showed her my I.D. and introduced myself. "The investigation's pretty confidential," I said, "so please don't tell anybody I was here."

The maid lowered her voice. "It's that son of hers, isn't it? Poor woman, never any peace. The boy was born from a bad seed." She dragged the yellow canvas bag into her lap and started rummaging through it. "Lord knows she's tried hard enough. Anything I can do to help. . . ."

"If you've got her address . . ."

"Poor Hilda. I'll have to call her. Here it is." She pulled out a dog-eared address book. "Do you need something to write with, honey?"

I already had a notepad and pencil in my hand.

"Good. We used to have coffee together in the mornings." She held the address book out the window for me to copy. "Sort of like taking a break. Twenty minutes or so for a chat. That's when she told me about her son."

I took down the address while she jabbered on, then broke in when she stopped for air.

"Thanks," I said. "You've been a lot of help, Miss—"

"Mrs. Benson. Eunice Benson, honey." She smiled at me with a full set of false teeth. "Anytime."

Before she could launch into another soliloquy, I started back across the lawn. But I stopped when I noticed I could see Martha Coyle's front door from the other house.

"Just one more thing," I said. "Have you ever seen this man next door?" I handed her Jake Murieta's picture, the one Noni gave me. She stared at it for a minute, then shook her head.

"I don't think so. Is he a delivery boy?"

"Sort of," I said, easing the picture out of her tight little grip. I thanked her again and left.

Back in the car I looked down at Hilda Gutierrez's address. She lived in Daly City. From here it would take a good thirty minutes to get there. Then I'd have to find the place. I checked my watch. It was a quarter to four. Not enough time.

Mrs. Gutierrez would have to wait. Right now, there was a lucky soul in line for a Tuxedo Message in the Berkeley Hills. I'd have to hurry if I wanted to change and deliver it on time.

39

The Tuxedo Message victim was a professor at Cal, a withered old man of about seventy, who was so moved that his Economics 301 class didn't want him to retire that I had to stop every few seconds so he could blow his nose and dab his eyes. When I finished, the whole class popped out from behind the bushes with champagne and cheers.

I tried to think of a single professor I'd had in college who I'd even consider doing such a thing for, but whenever I thought of any of them, all I could come up with were nasty little rhyming ditties that insulted them. Watching the kids mill around the old man, I wished I'd had just one teacher like him. Maybe I should have studied economics.

It was five thirty when I started back to the City. The freeway wasn't too congested: Most of the commuters were headed north and Daly City was south of San Francisco. But as soon as I crossed the bridge, things got clogged up fast. I puttered along in stop-and-go traffic for about twenty-five minutes before hitting the Interstate

280 turnoff. Then it took another twenty minutes to reach Daly City, and another fifteen to find the Gutierrez house.

It was up off the highway in a maze of ticky-tacky little houses that somebody wrote a song about once. They were all identical except for color. Mrs., and Mr. if there was one, Gutierrez had made a stab at individuality by painting their house pastel blue with white trim. The place next door was pale yellow with white trim, and the one across the street was just plain white. They all had a neat little patch of grass in front and a set of piney shrubs on either side of the door.

I parked across the street, pulled a sweater over my tuxedo top, then walked up to the door wondering if everybody inside these houses looked the same too. If I knocked on doors, would neat little families of four with pastel variations of skin and hair color come marching out?

I shook my head to clear it, then rang the doorbell to Mrs. Gutierrez's house. While I waited, three boys bicycled past and shouted at a bunch of girls roller-skating down the street. Of course the girls giggled and acted dumb. A few doors down, somebody's mother was calling her son, and somebody else's dog was yapping. A second, deeper bark joined in from somewhere down the street.

"Suburbia," I muttered under my breath, and thanked my landlord for giving me cheap rent above a saloon in North Beach. If I had to live in Daly City, I'd probably paint myself some pastel shade and end up with a glazed look in my eyes.

I turned back to the door when I heard the latch rattle. A short, stout woman with strong Mexican-Indian features filled the lower half of the doorway. The flat, angu-

lar features, thoughtful black eyes, and the gentle patience in her expression were the same I'd seen on the
faces of so many *Chicanos* of Indian heritage.

"Yes?" she asked, and wiped her hands on her apron.
It was the kind with a bodice, the kind grandmothers and
spinster aunts were supposed to wear.

"Are you Mrs. Gutierrez?"

"*¿Sí?*"

I pulled out my identification and held it up so that she
could read it. "My name's Ronnie Ventana. I'm a private
investigator and I'd like to ask you a few questions. Can I
come in?"

Her reaction wasn't what I'd expected. She looked
startled at first, then anxious. "Is it Manolo?" she asked.
There was a tremor in her voice. I couldn't figure out
what she was talking about until I remembered that Eunice Benson said there was a son who got in trouble a lot.

"This has nothing to do with your son, Mrs. Gutierrez.
I promise."

She didn't act like she believed me. Maybe it was just
because she figured it was only a temporary reprieve. The
bad news was bound to come someday. Her patient face
made me wonder how any son could cause her grief.

"I promise," I said again.

"*Bien.*" She shrugged, resigned, then stepped back to
let me in.

The living room was the size of a closet and it was
stuffed with all kinds of furniture. None of it matched,
but the wood and metal on every piece were polished to a
high gloss. Everything was immaculate. Pictures of saints
adorned the walls: the Virgin Mary with a fat baby cradled in her arms, Jesus Christ with a bright-red bleeding
heart and a cross of fire superimposed on his chest, and
some other people I didn't even recognize. There were

statues on every tabletop, and she'd set up some kind of altar in a corner with little votive candles all around it.

"Please, sit down," Mrs. Gutierrez said. "How may I help you?"

I picked a chair with little lace doilies draped over its arms. "I understand you worked for Judge Coyle."

She nodded. "Until I hurt my back. *Señorita* Coyle, she is not ill, is she?"

"No," I said, "she's fine, last I heard." I drew out Jake Murieta's picture and passed it across the table. "Have you ever seen this man before? Did he ever come to Judge Coyle's house?"

She took the snapshot, then picked up a pair of reading glasses from behind a ceramic nativity scene. As soon as she glanced down at the picture, she nodded.

"*Sí,*" she said. "*¡Cómo no!* He was a messenger, I think."

I fought to keep the excitement out of my voice. "A messenger? What kind of messenger?"

"I do not know. He would come, knock on the door, and say he came for the envelope. I would tell *Señorita* Coyle and she would give me a blue envelope. I would give it to him and he would go."

"Wasn't that sort of unusual?"

"*Señorita* Coyle, she used overnight mail many times."

"Was the address on the envelopes always the same?"

Mrs. Gutierrez looked confused. "Excuse me, *señorita*. What did you say?"

"The address on the envelope—did she send them to the same place every time?"

"There was no address," she said slowly, like she was picturing the blue envelopes in her mind.

"You're sure?"

She took off her reading glasses and dropped them in

her lap, then passed the picture back to me and nodded. She looked troubled. I leaned forward.

"Mrs. Gutierrez, do you have any idea what was in those envelopes? Did you ever look inside any of them?"

She sat up straight and lifted her chin. "I would never do such a thing."

"I didn't think you would," I said, "but I had to ask. When was the last time you saw this man? Did he come more than once?"

"*Sí*. He came every month, sometimes more. The last time he came was the week I resigned, the last week of March."

"And he took an envelope?"

"*Sí.*"

"Didn't you think it strange that a delivery boy was driving a Lincoln?"

She seemed unperturbed. "I did not think of these things."

"Mrs. Gutierrez, if you had to guess what was in those envelopes, what would you say it was?"

"I do not know."

"Did Judge Coyle ever mention anything to you about him or the envelopes, anything that might hint at what was going on between the two of them?"

The old woman shook her head again. "No, *nada.*"

A car door slammed outside. She heard it the same time I did and stood up.

"My husband," she announced.

I got up too. "Can we talk some more? Later maybe?"

"*Sí, ¡cómo no!* But later, not now."

I left my card, shook hands with Mr. Gutierrez on my way out, and drove back to the city with the fog rolling in behind me.

40

As soon as I got home, I looked up Jacobo Murieta in the phone book and dialed. I was lucky; Marina answered.

"This is Ronnie. Do you remember ever seeing your uncle bring home any blue envelopes?"

"Sure. All the time."

"Did you ever see what was in them?"

"Sure. He'd take them to his room, but one time I watched through the keyhole when my aunt was out. It was full of money. Loads of money. There was so much money in there that I borrowed a hundred dollars one time and he didn't even notice."

"Did you ever count it?"

"Are you kidding? He could have walked in on me."

"Anything else in there besides the money? Any letters or receipts or anything?"

"A piece of paper. He put it in his top bureau drawer and I went in later to look. It was just a piece of paper with somebody's name on it. He had a stack of them. I figured they paid him off, maybe for a hit or something."

"Do you remember any of the names?"

"Michael something. I don't know. You want to see them? I bet they're still there." The kid was too smart.

"That'd be great. I'll be right over."

"No, don't. My aunt's home. I'll meet you somewhere. Uh, how about the Saint Francis Soda Shop?"

"On Twenty-fourth and York? I'll be there in twenty minutes."

"Bring cigarettes," she said before she hung up.

I hated to contribute to the corruption of a minor, but what else could I do? Nobody else gave it away. I went into the bar downstairs, fed quarters into the cigarette machine, and picked out a couple of the lowest tar and nicotine packs I could find.

When I drove up to the soda shop, there was a group of about fifteen teenagers just hanging out on the corner. If I'd wanted a secret meeting, this wasn't going to be it. Marina waved from the middle of the group and crossed the sidewalk over to where I parked.

"Hiya," she said, then shot a look of triumph over her shoulder to the other kids. "Want to meet some of my friends?"

They were almost all dressed in leather and ankle boots, and the whole group pulsed to salsa blaring from a ghetto blaster on the sidewalk.

"Sure, why not?" I kicked off the engine and got out to mingle with the kids. Marina introduced me all the way around as "my friend, the private investigator." The boys acted like they didn't believe her, so she asked me to show them my I.D.—which I did. I owed the kid that much. The boys passed it around and tried to act like they saw P.I. I.D.'s every day. Marina just beamed.

After twenty minutes of chatting I figured I'd paid my dues. I pulled Marina aside. "Did you bring the papers?"

The whole group was watching her. "Sure," Marina said.

"All right. Let's take a look at them. In the car."

She followed me to the Citroën. "You can have them," she said when she pulled a little blue bundle out of her jacket pocket. "Here."

"I'll give them back," I promised. "Oh, I almost forgot." I handed her the two packs of cigarettes. "Make these your last two, okay?"

She took one look at them. "Low tar. Yuck!"

"You're welcome," I said. "I'll be in touch."

I left Marina with her buddies and their little party on the sidewalk. Nobody seemed to mind the noise they were making, and they weren't really looking for any trouble. Once you got over their tough-kid outfits, the leather and spiked hair, their faces all looked innocent enough. Kids were kids, be it in the *barrio* or Daly City, or even Pacific Heights.

41

The last person I expected to see when I reached the top of the stairs to my apartment was Philly Post, but there he was, big as life, looking sort of out of place and exposed away from his junky old desk and glassed-in office.

I stopped short when I saw him. He was sitting on the top step, just outside my door, and when he saw me, his face scrunched up in what I guess was supposed to be a smile. It could have passed for a scowl.

"Ventana," he said, and pushed himself off the stoop. "It's about time."

I glanced at my watch. Ten thirty. "Am I on curfew?"

"I can put you there if you want," he said.

"Did we have an appointment, or am I missing something? I don't remember—"

"You got any coffee inside?"

"Sure. So does the place downstairs."

He just nodded, so I stepped around him to the door. "How about a beer? I've got Anchor Steams in the fridge."

He stomped in after me. "Anchor's good."

Three paces put him in the middle of the room. He stopped and circled the tight space with his eyes while I dropped my jacket on the counter and fished two beers out of the fridge. "You live by yourself?"

"Yeah." I handed him a bottle. "How about you?"

"Yeah."

I waved at the couch and pulled the chair away from the table I use for a desk. "This business or pleasure?"

"A little of both."

I nodded, took a long swallow from the bottle, and waited.

"You still trying to nail August?"

"Not really."

"Good. Pete didn't do it. The autopsy report clears him. The floater was only dead two days when they pulled him out, and he's got an alibi for all day. You still working Murieta?"

I took another long pull of Anchor Steam and pretended I hadn't heard.

"Yeah, okay," he said after a minute. "It's all right with me. I don't care."

"Is that what you came to tell me?"

He set his empty bottle down on the floor next to his feet. "Why don't you quit trying to be so tough all the time?"

"Why don't you?"

He shrugged. "I'm here, aren't I?"

The man had a point. I let myself relax. "You're all right, Post," I said. "How about another beer?"

He shook his head and stood up, then took his empty over to the counter by the sink. "You eat yet?"

"No."

"Any place around here any good?"

I grinned. "Are you asking me out to dinner, Lieutenant?"

The flat lines around his mouth went slack, and I could have sworn his cheeks went pink. He made some kind of gruff noise deep in his throat. "We ought to talk about Murieta," he said casually.

"Fine," I said. "I'll have dinner with you, but I don't want to talk about him."

"Come on." He opened the door. "You'll change your mind."

We went down the street to Arnie's Pizza Palace and split a pepperoni with anchovies and mushrooms. He talked me into telling him about Murieta when he threatened to turn me in for impeding a police investigation. The way he said it made it sound like a threat, but his big, hairy eyebrows went up just long enough for me to catch a glint of humor in them.

He was being nice about it, so I decided I should be too. But that didn't mean giving him everything. I opted for the gloss-and-tell technique and just gave him the highlights. I left out all the important names I knew he'd flip a switch over.

"So you know Murieta was working steady for somebody, but you don't know who and you don't know what," Philly said when I finished. I don't think he believed me.

"That about sums it up."

"And there's nothing else?

"I've got some ideas, but I'm not ready to talk about them yet."

"Since when? Don't be careful on my account," he said. "You come up with anything on Wilson?"

"Nope."

"We did. Some pigeon told one of my boys that he and Murieta were seen together a week before he died."

I understood then. That's what he wanted to tell me. The two were tied together somehow, but they didn't know how. I sat back in my chair and tried to figure out his unreadable face. "What's with you, Post?"

"What do you mean?"

"First you tell me to keep off the case, then you feed me little pieces of what you've got, and sic me on it. What gives?"

He thought about it for a minute, then said, "You're like a terrier after a rat. It takes a lot for you to let go. But you're smart, too, and that makes it even better. You ever heard of aikido?"

"It's some kind of martial art, like karate, isn't it?"

"It's a martial art, all right, but it's not like karate. It's not aggressive. With aikido you use the attacker's momentum to throw him off balance. You save your own energy that way."

"And you're just saving your energy?"

He shrugged. "My ego's not too big to live with. If you want to work this case for free, who am I to say you can't? I've got fifty other cases for you when this one's done." His eyebrows went up again and I saw the twinkle in his eyes. He was laughing hard inside, I could tell.

I grinned at him. "I'm your patsy on this one, Post, because it suits me. The terms on the next ones are negotiable."

"Sounds fair. Just call in the Mounties when you're ready."

"Right." The boy brought our pizza. I figured the business part of the meal was over. "Have you always lived by yourself?"

He tore the biggest slice away from the pie, folded it in

half, Italian style, and took a huge bite, then shook his head and swallowed. He ate like a greedy Doberman, huge gulps of food that he didn't even bother to chew.

"Used to be married," he said. "What about yourself?"

"I tried it."

He swallowed the rest of the slice and reached for another piece. "My ex watched too much TV. She figured I should be able to wrap up a case in an hour. Hour and a half at the most. She just couldn't get past the overtime."

"You do a lot of that?"

He inhaled his second wedge before he answered. "Sure. Why shouldn't I put in hours? That's what I get paid for." He reached for a third slice. "Why'd you split up?"

"It went kind of like a country-western song. He cheated. I cheated. We broke up. He's a good guy, I just couldn't live with him."

One of the marriage counselors said my fierce demand for loyalty was because my parents' early death had somehow screwed me up. When I asked him if his wife had ever cheated on him, he shifted uncomfortably in his big leather swivel chair and wouldn't meet my gaze for the rest of the hour. Even though Mitch kept seeing him, I refused to go back. Instead I went out, had my own affair, and made sure Mitch knew about it.

"What about Coogan?"

"What about him?"

"You seeing him, or what?"

"We're friends." I hesitated. "Blackie told me about the time you busted him."

"Yeah? Did he tell you he put the pimp in the hospital?"

"As a matter of fact no. He's still pretty upset about it."

Post scowled. "Coogan's an ass. The pimp pressed charges and talked the kid into it too. What were my choices? I made damn sure that pimp changed his mind, though, and the boy's too. I sent the kid home, but you know how that goes. He was back in a week. Coogan must think I'm God if he blames me for that."

There was one last piece of pizza left on the tray. I had a slice on my plate that I hadn't even touched.

"You want another one?" he asked. When I shrugged, he said, "Let's make it straight anchovies this time."

He walked me back to the apartment when we finished the second pizza, and we split my last beer before he left.

I sat on the couch a long time thinking after he was gone. Blackie wouldn't approve, but the more I saw of Philly Post, the more I thought he might just be okay.

After I brushed my teeth and slipped into a baggy old sweatshirt I use for a nightgown, I remembered the blue packet Murieta's niece had given me. It was still tucked safely in the bottom of my purse. I pulled it out and took it over to the table, turned on the lamp, and sat down.

The top of each blue page was sliced off, probably the letterhead. In the middle of every one of them was printed a name, in black ink. They were all men's names and they were all different. I read the first one aloud.

"Howard Glass." The name didn't mean a thing to me. I paged through the rest: Mark Jacobsen, John Ford, Kenneth Reston, Newton Placer, Robert Treebridge, Orville Bekins, Tom Wright, Leon MacMillan, and Keith Coleman. Ten in all. And none of them sounded familiar.

I fished out the list Blackie had copied at Judge Marks's house. None of the names matched the ones on the blue sheets. I checked the phone book. There were a few listings under some of the names, and none for the rest. The names weren't one-of-a-kind names, but they weren't that common either.

I put the papers back in my purse, opened the sofa bed, and crawled under the covers. There was nothing else I could do tonight.

42

In the morning I did my run, showered and dressed, then dialed the Hall of Justice.

"Yeah?" There was only a hint of the friendly tone from last night in Philly Post's voice when he picked up the phone. I heard voices talking in the background, so maybe he was trying to impress somebody with how tough he was.

"It's Ronnie," I said.

"What do you want?"

"Did I catch you at a bad time? I—"

"No. Go ahead. I've got a minute."

"This could take more than a minute. I've got a problem."

"Hold on." I heard him ask some people named Jim and Dave if he could have a moment. A door closed, and then Post came back on the line. "Okay."

"Will you run a list of names through your computer for me?"

"Depends. Is this Murieta?"

"Sort of." There was a long pause at the other end.

"It's only ten names," I said, and wondered if I'd have to beg.

More silence, then finally, "Let's have them."

I read them off and he took them down. "Where'd you get these?" he asked when I'd finished.

"A friend."

"Hmmph! It'd better be. It won't do either of us any good if they're from a B and E. I'll call you back."

He hung up and I sat there a minute feeling proud of myself. Four days ago Post wouldn't even have taken my call, much less a request like that.

I stuck around and ate breakfast, waiting for him to call back, then, after killing an hour without hearing from him, decided to drive over to Diamond Heights.

Noni Witherspoon was home. She opened the door wearing a flowered silk caftan and pink marabou slippers. There were boxes all over the place, and the tops of shelves and tables had all been cleared.

"Moving?"

She nodded. "I can't afford the apartment without Jake."

I said yes when she offered me a cup of coffee and waited for her to sit at the table on the terrace before I pulled out my list.

"I've got some names I'd like you to look at. Tell me if you recognize any of them."

"Of course." Noni glanced down at the sheet I scooted across the table to her. Her arched eyebrows puckered and her pouting lips moved as she read over the list, stopping at each name with a forced show of concentration. When she finished, she pushed the list back across to me and wrapped her delicate little fingers around her china cup.

"I'm sorry," she said. "I don't think Jake ever mentioned any of them. Who are they?"

"Remember that judge you told me about?" Noni nodded. "She gave these to him. He made a separate trip for each one. That means he went there ten times. Are you sure he didn't say more about her?"

She passed a hand across her forehead, the damsel in distress. Was she taking acting lessons or what? "I can't remember. What does it mean?"

I shrugged. "That's hard to say. You're my first stop. Any thoughts?"

Again the forced show of concentration, but this time she cheated, she took a sip of coffee while she pretended to think.

"Jake never talked about business to me. He didn't think women should worry about money and work and things. He wanted me to quit Manion's, but I said I wouldn't unless he married me." Her eyes brimmed with tears. "I miss him so much."

I pushed a box of tissues from my side of the table toward Noni and waited while she plucked one out and sniffed into it. Then I leaned forward.

"What if I told you that his niece said he was a hit man, that he carried out contracts?"

She stiffened. "I don't believe it," she said, but her protest didn't fool either of us.

"So you knew."

"What difference does it make? He was good to me. He treated me like a princess." Noni sighed. "I'll never find anybody like him again." She started to cry all over again. I'd taken all I could, so I stood up.

"If you think of anything, give me a call," I said, but I didn't think she would. I saw myself out and left Noni dabbing at her eyes.

About three blocks away I found a corner grocery with a pay phone. I called Edna up at the parole office in Oakland and asked her to punch the names into her computer. I spelled each of them out for her. We were halfway through the list before something turned up.

"Robert Treebridge," Edna said. "Here. I've got him."

"Terrific. What's it say?"

"Nothing." Edna sounded baffled.

"What do you mean 'nothing'?"

"There's nothing here, just his name. That means either he's been pardoned or he's dead. Let me see if he's in this other file." She talked while she punched. "I heard from Dirty Harry yesterday. He loves Arizona."

"What's he doing there?"

"Didn't he tell you? He's spending the summer at a dude ranch."

"Harry?"

"Mm-hmm. Something about a secret dream to be a cowboy."

I laughed out loud when I tried to picture my stodgy old ex-boss riding a roundup.

"Sorry, Ronnie. No more on Treebridge."

There was nothing on the rest either. I thanked her and hung up. I struck out with Aldo too. He wasn't even in, so I drove over to Spanish Heaven to see what Rogelio knew.

The restaurant was crammed. The usual lunchtime crowd filled the plain Formica-topped tables, and a line overflowed to the sidewalk outside. Business was good.

When Rogelio saw me, he waved a spatula in greeting and served me a couple of tamales to keep me busy while he manned the kitchen for the throng outside. When the line finally disappeared and the tables were nearly empty, he turned the kitchen over to his aunt.

"Veronica, *¿qué pasa?*"

I told him what I wanted while he opened the back door to cool out the kitchen. He leaned up against the doorjamb and held his hand out for the list.

"Let me see."

He went over it, then shook his head.

"These are not *compadres,* Veronica. They are all Anglo."

"I know. But Murieta is somehow tied to them, and nobody seems to have heard of them before. I thought you might have."

He shook his handsome head again. "I will ask," he said. "I will do what I can." He sent me on my way with a CARE package: a couple of cheese burritos "for tonight."

43

I ate half of one burrito on the drive down to Daly City and wished I hadn't. The tamales had been more than enough. Mid-afternoon traffic was light, practically nonexistent. Mrs. Gutierrez was home, cleaning her own house and looking happy about it. At least until she saw me.

"*Señorita* Coyle, she is not in trouble, is she?" she asked when she opened the door.

"She could be," I said, and pulled out the list of names as I followed her inside. "I don't want to take up a lot of your time, but have you ever heard Judge Coyle mention any of these people? I don't know in what context, maybe for a party or business or something."

Mrs. Gutierrez laid down her dustrag and crossed the cluttered living room to a sewing basket at the foot of a dumpy-looking upholstered chair in the corner. She pulled out her reading glasses and sat down to go over the list.

Her old-fashioned wire-framed glasses fit perfectly with her bibbed and ruffled apron. She ought to be baking gingerbread cookies and cupcakes for rosy-cheeked children, I thought. Then she looked up.

"I'm sorry, *Señorita* Ventana. I do not recognize any of them." She handed the list back. "Are they friends of *Señorita* Coyle?"

"I don't know." I pulled out one of the pages Murieta's niece had given me. "What about this? Do you recognize this stationery?"

Mrs. Gutierrez took the paper. "I have seen paper like this, yes. *Señorita* Coyle, she uses this paper to write her personal letters. Her letters are bigger, though."

"Engraved at the top?"

"*Sí, sí.* With her name and address."

"I think someone cut the top off," I said. "See how that edge is sharper than the other three? What do you think?"

Mrs. Gutierrez ran her finger along the upper edge and nodded.

"That page was in one of the envelopes Judge Coyle gave the man whose picture I showed you yesterday. There are nine other sheets with nine other different names on them."

Mrs. Gutierrez shook her head and handed the page back to me. "I am sorry again. I cannot help. I do not know why *Señorita* Coyle gave envelopes to that man. I do not know who he is. I thought he was a messenger. *Señorita* Coyle never spoke to him, never saw him. She never came to the door when he was there. She would have if he was important."

There had to be something this woman could tell me, something that would put me on the right track.

"What was it like working for her? What kind of person is she?" I asked.

Mrs. Gutierrez studied me for a full minute, then

seemed to figure I was all right. "She was hard," she said, "very *formál* all the time. I"—she gestured at her apron and dress—"I am neat, but never could I be neat enough for the *señorita*. I would clean the living room one way and she would tell me to do it another. If I moved one object in the house, she would know. Always she would tell me to move it back. She is very smart, the *señorita*, but I think there are better ways to use such a brain than to worry about such small things. That is for the house-keeper, for me."

"How long did you work for her?"

"Five years and one month. I thought she would change, grow accustomed to my ways and I to hers, but no. She never changed. She was hard, very hard. That is why, when I hurt my back, my husband said, 'Stay home.' He says thirty-five years of work is enough. He will retire next month and we will see the country then, visit our children and our grandchildren. Here they are." She opened a little scrapbook on the table next to the Bible and pulled out a couple of pictures. The grandkids.

I asked her about them, admired their photographs, then wished her well, thanked her, and left. When I got back to the apartment, the answering machine was blinking like a lucky star. The only message on it was from Marina. She wanted me to call her.

44

I called Marina back, but nobody was home. I hung up and dialed the Hall of Justice. Nobody was home there, either, at least not in Post's office.

I dropped the phone into its cradle and picked up the bio sheet on Martha Coyle. I tossed it, along with the blue packet of stationery, on my work table and stared at it for a long time. That's when I noticed it took Judge Coyle five years to get through law school. I reached for the phone again.

"Aldo, do me a favor. Go talk to your friend, you know, the one on the third floor who clerks for one of the judges."

"Judge Harris?"

"Whoever. Ask her to find out if Martha Coyle worked her way through law school."

"How's she going to know that?"

"I don't know, Aldo. Just ask."

"What are we finding out?"

"I'm not exactly sure. It took her five years to earn a three-year law degree. I'm just curious. Call me back."

I hung up and let my eyes wander to the window. My friend, the Chinese lady across the street, was taking in her laundry. There was someone in the apartment with her, and while she talked over her shoulder to him, her sing-songy Chinese voice carried across to me.

The place was a far cry from the big Sausalito house I'd shared with Mitch—no pool or tennis courts here. And no hot tub either. But the strange thing was, I liked this place better. It felt more like home than Sausalito ever did.

Mitch had always joked about me being from the wrong side of the tracks, but in a way he was right. Crossing them had been interesting, but this was home. I was living my life the way I wanted, doing what felt right.

All of a sudden I remembered the beer I'd picked up on my way home. It was bound to make the waiting a little easier. I pulled one out of the fridge, and the phone rang. I jumped on it.

"Hello?"

"Hey, doll, what's up? You didn't leave your machine on last night."

"Why didn't you tell me you put that pimp in the hospital?"

"What pimp?" Blackie asked. "Am I on the right train?"

"When Philly Post busted you over that runaway case, you put the pimp in the hospital."

"Oh, that. Shit. He was in for a couple of days, no big deal. What's it got to do with anything?"

"Post convinced him to drop the charges—that's why they were dropped."

"He tell you that?"

"Yes."

"And you're gonna go with it?"

"Don't be so jaded, Blackie. Listen, I can't talk. Post and Aldo are supposed to call me back."

Blackie snorted. "Aren't you thick? Five bucks says he won't."

"Post?"

"Yeah."

"You're on."

"Yeah?" He sounded baffled by my confidence. "Don't get too cocky, doll. He's bound to yank you."

"He's not so bad."

"Sure, sure. I'll be by tomorrow to collect."

"You mean deliver."

He snorted again and hung up. After I picked up my beer from the kitchen counter, I thought of Mrs. Gutierrez. I set the can down, found her number, and dialed.

"I'm sorry to bother you again, Mrs. Gutierrez, but I've got another question for you."

"*Señorita* Ventana." She sounded patient and warm. "I will try to help. As long as it helps *Señorita* Coyle."

I wasn't sure when, or how, Mrs. Gutierrez decided Martha Coyle was in trouble or that I was helping her out, but it seemed to be working for me, so I wasn't about to set her straight.

"Do you know if Judge Coyle worked her way through law school?"

"She never spoke of such things." I could tell she was bewildered but was too polite to ask why I wanted to know. I tried a different tack.

"While you worked for her, did her family ever visit? Her parents or anybody like that?"

"Ah, *sí*. Her father and mother, they are very nice. *Muy buena gente, muy amable.* So different and relaxed.

To work for them would be a dream. But their servants, they are so happy, they would never leave."

If her parents had servants, they had money. It wasn't likely their darling daughter had to take leave in the middle of law school to earn tuition. Besides, if she needed to, Judge Coyle was bright. There were such things as scholarships.

"Was she ever married, do you know?"

"No. But *Señor* August, he is her boyfriend. He is so handsome. Like you, he is an investigator. Do you know him?" She sighed. "Together, they are beautiful."

I wondered how beautiful Mrs. Gutierrez would think they were if she saw them getting their jollies with whips and bindings the way I had the other night. "Thank you so much, Mrs. Gutierrez. I'll try not to bother you any more."

Aldo called back as soon as I hung up.

"She was on medical leave," he said. "I checked her personnel file, and it says she went on medical leave a month into her second year."

"For two years?"

"That's what it said. Listen, Ronnie, you can't tell anybody how you found out, okay? I could get fired for this."

"Were there any medical records in the file? Anything that said what she was doing those two years?"

"Ronneeeeee—"

"Don't whine, Aldo. Were there?"

"No. Why is this so important?"

"I'm not sure. But thanks, Aldo. I owe you one."

It wasn't until after I hung up that I realized Aldo had coughed up without angling for a date—lunch or otherwise. He hadn't even tried. And come to think of it, when I mentioned talking to the clerk upstairs, he more or less jumped on it. Hmmm. I smiled. "Aldo, you old dog. Are you getting over me?"

My beer was warm by now, but I finished it anyway. I tried Marina again, but there was still no answer. As I dumped the empty in the waste can under the sink, I considered calling Philly Post back, but decided not to push. He could just cut me off if I got impatient. After all, he was doing me a favor. And from the way Blackie talked, that in itself was a miracle—close to an act of God. Why push it? Besides, it would blow my bet with Blackie.

One thing was certain, though. Judge Martha Coyle was suddenly at the top of my "further investigation" list. Her strange notes to Murieta, even her association with him to begin with, was too weird. No, she needed looking at—close up and firsthand. The kind that only gets done after dark, in empty houses.

I opened the top of the laundry hamper in the closet and had to smile when I remembered the Riley burglar alarm. After rummaging through the crumpled clothes I found what I wanted: the black jeans I'd worn the other night. Before I could put them on, though, the phone rang. It had to be Philly Post. But it wasn't.

"Do you do messages?" the voice on the other end asked. "Do you do them in a tux?"

How did Myra ever get anything done? "Yes."

"Can you do one today?"

I glanced at my watch. It was just after five o'clock. "That depends. When and where?"

"I was hoping for six thirty. I'll pay double," the man on the phone said.

Martha Coyle would have to wait. And so would Philly Post—if he ever called.

45

Since I had to go to Marin to deliver the message, I stopped off afterward at Mitchell's house to trade cars. The cop who had warned me last week didn't impress me as one with a memory.

Mitch was home, still harping about Skipper's human relations job, so I didn't want to stay, but when he offered me a beer, I accepted anyway.

We sat in his living room with all the furniture he'd picked out after we broke up—high-tech classical stuff—surrounded by modern art and open glass and stared beyond the redwoods to the quiet, glistening lights of Marin below.

"Human relations, Ron. Think about it. You could do all kinds of shit, know what I mean?"

I took a sip of beer. "Uh-uh."

"Skipper says you'd be interviewing people to hire them and doing a little background investigating on them, you know, making sure they don't have any problems they aren't telling you about. Man, Ronnie, you're a natural for this. All you've got to do is pick up the phone and you can be pulling in forty K, steady and solid."

He sat back in his white leather upholstered chair and sort of spread his arms out. The body language said what he hadn't: "You could have all this too!"

I sighed. Poor Mitchell was so hot for his yuppie-scum life-style, he couldn't see past the Jasper Johns artwork on his walls.

"Thanks, Mitch. Like I said before, I think I'll pass."

He mumbled something vaguely acquiescent, but I wasn't fooled. I knew I'd be hearing about it again.

My beer glass was still half full, so I changed the subject to something I knew we wouldn't argue about. We talked about stuff like my running, his soccer league, his planned bid for partner at the firm, and how busy Myra's Tuxedo Messages were keeping me.

The twilight was easy and comfortable between us, and for a while I almost forgot how much we'd hurt each other a long time ago. We watched the sun go down, opened a couple more beers, and before I realized what I was doing, I found myself telling him about the Fort Point murder case. I told him how Murieta hadn't really died the day I saw him, but actually two days later; how he was connected to the woman judge who'd gained fame during the Russian Hill rapist trial; and how Pete August was somehow the bridge between the two.

Mitchell listened to the whole disjointed story without saying a word, his blue eyes hidden by the shadows of dusk and his long, slightly bowed legs stretched out in front of him.

"Right now I'm working on the judge," I told him. "She was giving Murieta money and the names of some people I'm having tracked down. Since he was a professional hit man—"

"Christ, Ronnie! Do you really want to hang out with this class of people all your life?"

I'd been over and over the same turf with Mitch a hundred times before. There was no point rehashing it one more time. If he ever learned to let go, to just accept me as I am, then he'd be the man of my dreams, the guy I thought I'd married. And maybe he felt the same way about me, who knows?

But neither one of us was going to change. Neither one of us wanted to. And I had the uneasy feeling that if we did, it was much too late to matter anyhow.

I set my empty glass down on the table and stood. Mitch rose, too, looking surprised, but not contrite.

"It's been nice talking to you, Mitch. Until now. I think I'd better go."

It was after eight o'clock when I got home. As I started up the stairs to my apartment, I wondered if Philly Post was up there waiting for me like he'd been the other night. He wasn't, though, and the little twinge of disappointment I felt surprised me. Was it because I wanted the poop on the list I gave him, or was it something else? "Philly Post?" I said out loud, then shook my head and pulled out my keys. "No way."

The phone-message indicator was blinking, so I rewound the tape and played it back. Eight calls and every time the caller had hung up without leaving a message. No words, just silence, a dial tone, and eight loud beeps.

I changed, packed my stuff in my little black bag, filled a Thermos with coffee, and headed out the door. It was eight thirty and the sun had just gone down when I pulled up on Vallejo Street.

The lights at 2640 were on, second level up front, probably a bedroom. I edged the Toyota to the curb a few

houses down, bent the side-view mirror so that I could
see the house in it, and slouched down in the seat to wait.

It was best to break into a house between six and ten at
night because most people were gone then—if they were
going out. If Martha Coyle was in for the evening, I'd
have to come back tomorrow night. Either that or violate
cat-burglar rule number one: Don't ever break into a
house when somebody's home.

I poured myself a cup of coffee and settled in for a
long, cozy wait while the evening fog rolled in. I fixed my
eyes on the side-view mirror and watched.

At a quarter to nine the lights upstairs went out. I sat
up. A few seconds later a light came on downstairs, then
one in the garage. As I watched, the garage door tilted
open with a slow-motion hum I could hear even with my
window rolled up.

Martha Coyle stepped out into the garage in a pair of
slacks and a red leather jacket. She walked over behind
the car parked inside and bent over. I got so excited, my
breath fogged the window. I had to roll it down to see
what she was doing.

When I caught sight of her again, she was pulling a
helmet over her head. In the empty night I heard a soft
purr, then watched as she curved out from behind the car
and disappeared down the street on a motorcycle.

The light in the garage went off and the door started to
drop with a slow, lumbering pulse. I ditched my coffee
cup on the floor, grabbed my bag, and scrambled out of
the car.

I made it by inches, shoving the bag in first in front of
me, then rolling my body flat beneath the door just seconds before it swung shut. It had to be the easiest break-
in I'd done—except for the time I just walked in through
the open patio door of a house in Walnut Creek. I'd have

to save the Riley for another night, some night when I could take my time and do it just for the sheer pleasure.

I pushed myself up off the hard cement floor, my eyes adjusting to the semidarkness. I stood frozen to one spot, smelling the faint filling-station odors from the car: gas and oil mixed with the vague, clean scent of new-car upholstery. I blinked and looked around.

The late-model maroon Mercury took up most of the garage. There was precious little else inside—a broom, a set of skis and poles along one wall, and a tiny porthole window along another.

I felt my way carefully to the door and knocked. There could still be someone inside. No one answered, but I had to move fast. Martha Coyle could come humming back on her Kawasaki any minute.

Two steps led up to the door that gave into the house. I slipped on a pair of gloves, reached for the knob and turned it, then exhaled when the door gave. I knew it would. Everybody thought a garage door was as safe as any other door in the house, so they never wired it in as part of the security system. They never locked it either. Their mistake. That kind of setup was like an engraved invitation to come in and browse.

I pushed open the door gently, then stepped into a big open space that smelled of onions and bread. It had to be the kitchen. Two empty TV-dinner trays were stacked on the counter with an empty wine goblet next to them. So much for the high life.

I flicked the flashlight off and on as I tiptoed down the hall, peeking into every dark doorway I passed: laundry room, dining room, living room. The place was pretty big. I snuck into the study and was half thankful that it was lit by a street lamp just outside the window. It meant I could see pretty well, but it also meant I couldn't use my penlight unless I pulled the curtains. The problem with that was, there weren't any.

I checked out the rest of the room. Studded leather chairs, English-fox-hunt paintings on the walls, and one side of the room done in wall-to-wall bookshelves. The view was fantastic: the Bay, Angel Island, and both bridges. The desk was one of those antique mahogany monsters from the eighteen hundreds, the kind the president always sits behind when he wants to look official. It was perfect for a judge.

I sat down at the desk, stifled my conscience, and pulled open the lap drawer. Everything was stacked in neat little piles and compartments: pens, pencils, stamps, envelopes, and stationery. Blue, with her name and address engraved at the top. Everything looked hot off the counters of the nearest office-supply store.

I shut the drawer and noticed a thick leather-bound volume on the corner of the desk, just off the edge of the leather blotter. I picked it up, angled it toward the lamp light, and read the gold lettering on the cover: "Records."

Every page had a heading centered at the top: "Home," "Taxes," "Investments," "Medical." On the left was the subheading "Description," and on the right, "Location."

I read the first lines under "Home:" "Mortgage." To the right of it, in the other column, was "safe deposit." Next to "Home Improvements," was "file cabinet, third drawer."

I squinted into the shadows, and sure enough, there was a big oak file cabinet over in the corner, between the bookcases and the window. Next I flipped to the "Medical" heading. There was just one listing under it: "File, lower dresser drwr., bdrm."

Great. Rule number two for any cat burglar was: Never get boxed in, like on the second story of a residence. I really would have preferred to stay downstairs, but I knew I didn't always get what I wanted, so I had a hook and rope in my bag in case I needed to slide out a second-story window. After all, weren't rules made to be broken?

I folded the book shut, picked up my bag, and tiptoed upstairs, listening the whole time for motorcycles down the street and garage doors humming open. At the top of the stairs I poked my head in the first doorway I came to. It was a bedroom, practically empty and obviously unused. The next room had more furniture, but it was basically the same.

There were three more doors. One was to a bathroom and the other two to bedrooms. They were plusher and better furnished than the first two. The plushest one had to be Martha Coyle's. I stepped inside: gilt-edged antiques, a king-sized four-poster—the better to tie her lovers to—and embroidered drapes. House beautiful.

I checked the bathroom to make sure nobody was hiding in it, then flashed my penlight into the closet. Wool suits and dresses, a couple of ski parkas, a couple of white karate pajamas, and about fifteen pairs of shoes. There was a shelf full of sweaters on the right and another set of skis and poles stacked on the left.

I crossed over to the window and closed the drapes. Even though I wasn't confident enough to turn on the overhead light, at least I could use the penlight without worrying about being spotted from the outside.

The dresser was across from the bed—a tall highboy with the look and feel of solid cherry. Nothing second-class in this house.

The bottom drawer was jammed, but I yanked and it

gave. The whole thing was crammed full of yellow manila folders. I sat down cross-legged on the fluffy carpet and reached in for one off the top.

"Nineteen eighty-five" was scrawled across the front in broad red-ink letters. The folder was about half an inch thick with a photocopied cover letter stapled to the inside front cover. I skimmed it. It was a request for copies of all her medical records for that year. I rummaged through the other folders, and they all had the same kind of letter. But they only went back to 1979. Nothing even close to when she'd been in law school.

I turned back to the folder in my lap. There was about half an inch worth of photocopied reports in it, and they all looked like the same doctor wrote them. The dates were in fourteen- or fifteen-day intervals starting with the one on top from January and ending with November and December in the back. I skimmed the pages, trying to decipher the doc's handwriting. It was tough. I could make out the words *mood* and *relationships* on some of the pages, but basically there was nothing too legible or too exciting. In the back he started talking about aggression versus assertiveness, and something about some kind of hang-up with family relationships.

The last few pages had a different format and they were typed. *Pt. announced today will no longer seek therapy. States is ready to deal with her trauma in the way she feels is appropriate. Dr. offered to facilitate further but Pt. declined. It is the opinion of this Dr. that Pt. has her response well in hand and is capable of further resolution on her own.*

The rest showed she'd seen a different doctor in April for the flu and she had a gynecological exam two months later. The last page said she had vaccinations against hepatitis and malaria—probably for a trip someplace overseas. I set the folder on the floor and pulled out a couple more: one from four years ago and a skinny one from 1979.

I went for the thin one. There were only a couple of pages from the shrink in it, and they were both from December, the third and eighteenth. At the top of the December third page was the heading "Initial Visit." I read what I could make out.

Pt. female thirty-nine years of age. Occ: judge, prior, prosecutor. Pt. suffers occasional acute anxieties resulting from traumatic experience in her past. Pt. not ready to disclose nature of trauma, only that it occurred during law school.

I skimmed the next report for the word *trauma*. She still hadn't spilled it. I checked the 1980 folder and went halfway into 1981. Martha Coyle talked to her shrink about everything, it seemed: how she couldn't find a "suitable man" to date, remodeling her kitchen (I made a mental note to take a closer look on my way out), how she resented her married sister with three kids, and how she wanted more out of her job. I had to work through all of that garbage before she finally got to the heart of the matter—the trauma.

Fourteen visits into 1981 she finally told her shrink what was on her mind: rape. Specifically her own. There it was, all in black and white. And even though I couldn't make out all the words, I got enough out of it to get the gist of what happened to Judge Coyle her second year at law school.

One night on her way home from the law library her car broke down. Four guys stopped to help her, offered to drive her home, then took her to a park instead. They raped her over and over again until the sun came up. Then they beat her and left her for dead. A birdwatcher found her, barely breathing, naked from the waist down, half drowned at the bottom of a ravine.

They never caught the four guys, never prosecuted them. The family attorney advised her family not to pursue it because Martha Coyle couldn't remember anything about her attackers except that they were white and in their early twenties.

I forced myself to keep reading. Weeks after the hospital released her she signed up for every self-defense class she could find. I couldn't blame her. She took karate and kung fu and got black belts in both of them. But she still woke up with nightmares every night and lived every day in anger and fear.

In the shrink's opinion she should have followed up and prosecuted the guys. That way she'd come to terms with what happened. "Closure" was what the shrink called it. I understood now why she'd taken the two years off. Two years didn't seem quite enough after what she'd been through.

A wave of nausea swept over me. I shut the folder, picked up the others, and stuffed them all back where I'd found them.

I suddenly felt ashamed. What I'd read was nobody's business but Martha Coyle's and her doctor's. I started to get up, then remembered Mrs. Maximum Marks. She'd been raped too. Was there a connection? It was possible, but I doubted it. The two assaults had happened years apart.

I got up and opened the drapes, made sure everything in the room was the same way I'd found it, then retraced my steps and left through the front door.

Back in the car I glanced at the dash. Midnight. I'd been up there for over three hours. And those three hours left me feeling nothing but admiration for Martha Coyle.

She was a survivor. And one thing was certain, I thought as I put the car into gear, Martha Coyle wouldn't go creeping around at night snooping into other people's private lives. Sometimes being a P.I. just wasn't worth it.

At home I stripped, took a long, steaming shower, drank a beer, and read my Japanese primer until the sun came up. Then, and only then, did I fall asleep.

46

It was almost ten when I woke up and went for a run. I ran for an hour and a half just to clear my head. It was close to noon when I finally got around to checking my phone messages.

Philly Post's call was conspicuously absent. Two Tuxedo Message requests, both birthdays, I set up for next week. Myra'd be back by then. There was nothing I could do about the three hang-ups—calls with no messages.

I dawdled around with errands, taking old newspapers down to the recycling center instead of just leaving them at the dumpster where they'd be picked up, and dropping my clothes off at the laundry, then going grocery shopping. Most of the stuff I could have done anytime, but I wanted to do them now. I needed the comfort of being on automatic pilot. I wanted to feel as good as people who go to work nine-to-five, people who didn't have to face hard choices or have regrets. I didn't want to think.

It was one o'clock when I finished piddling around and stopped at the bar downstairs for a beer. No way around it, I had to look at the facts. But it was hard. I kept coming around to one important point: Nobody had hired me. I didn't need to follow up on any of it. Judgment told me to leave it alone, but instinct pushed me to keep after it. I ordered another beer, then another.

"Where'd you get those names?"

I looked up and was shocked to see Lieutenant Philly Post. "What are you doing here?"

He pulled out a chair and sort of fell into it. "Why don't you answer your phone? I must have listened to that damned recording fifteen times."

The hang-ups. "I think it was more like eight. Want a beer?" I asked.

"No, thanks." That meant it was strictly business.

I signaled the bartender to bring me another beer anyway. He brought an Anchor Steam and took away my empty. As I poured it out in a trickle against the side of my glass, I said, "Let me guess. You were in the neighborhood."

"I came down here for a specific piece of information, Ventana. We can chat some other time. Where'd you get those names?"

I set the empty next to the glass and noticed the angular planes of his face. Like this, in the semidarkness of the bar, he looked not exactly handsome, but at least interesting.

"A kid gave them to me," I said.

"Murieta's niece?"

"Lucky guess."

"Where'd she get them?"

"Why is this so important all of a sudden? Yesterday you were dragging your feet, doing me a big favor. Now you're all over me like lice on a cat."

"The guys on the list," he said. "They're all dead."

"Oh." Somehow that didn't surprise me, but I had the

feeling he thought it should. He was watching me so close he made me squirm. I forced a laugh. "Don't look at me, I didn't kill them."

"I didn't say you did." He drilled his eyes into me a couple of seconds more, then said, "Got any ideas?"

I gave him my best "nobody here but us chickens" look and shrugged. "Gee, I don't know. What about you?"

I could tell he didn't buy it, but he didn't push. "There's something strange about this list," he said. "These guys, every single one of them, were put away on rape charges. They all got out early for good behavior, and they all got popped within six months of getting out."

"I call that a real coincidence."

"It's more than coincidence, it's a pattern."

"Why are you so interested all of a sudden?" I took a long swig of beer, then raised my hand. "No, no, don't explain. I know you guys only look at *real* homicides. When some scummy ex-con gets popped, you just figure somebody did you a favor, right? But when it turns out to be ten, maybe twelve, murders, then you smell a promotion, is that it?"

"That's below the belt, Ventana. Your beer's talking for you." He scooted his chair back and made a motion to get up.

"Where are you going?" I asked.

"Where do you think? Back to my office to wait for the boys to bring in the Murieta girl."

"She won't talk to cops."

He dropped back into his chair, and I realized he hadn't intended to leave in the first place.

"You going to talk to her?" he asked.

"Sure. I'll probably see her."

"All right, here's what you do. Tell her we're all right. Tell her she can talk to us. That she'd better talk to us."

"Can't you cops talk to anybody without threats? This kid isn't going to come to you wagging her tail like some little puppy dog. She's tough. And she knows how cops operate."

"Tell her we only want justice served. We're just trying to find out who killed her uncle."

"Then she'll know I'm lying."

Philly showed his teeth and chuckled. He put both hands, palms down on the table, and pushed himself up. "All right. Tell her whatever you want. Just get her ass down to the Hall ASAP."

I saluted his retreating back. "Aye, aye, sir," I said, and flagged the bartender for a cup of coffee. When he brought it, I took it upstairs and drank it while I called Marina.

I got the aunt instead. Mrs. Murieta said her niece was in summer school. I almost said, "I bet," but bit my tongue and told her I'd call later. Then I went back downstairs and pulled the old blue Toyota out of the garage and headed for the Mission district.

After cruising with the low-riders for about an hour, I began to pick up on some of the salsa blaring out of the bouncing cars. It wasn't too bad, once you got used to it.

I found Marina on a corner near Valencia and Sixteenth. She was with two other girls, one with bleached-blond hair the color of weak beer and the other with a fringed suede leather jacket. Marina was wearing white go-go-type boots, black tights, and a sweat shirt so big and worn she must have dug it out of her dead uncle's closet. Fifteen was a tough age.

I pulled over in the bus zone and honked. Marina

didn't notice me until the bleached blonde looked over and I signaled at her to get Marina's attention. She caught Marina's eye, then jutted her chin out in my direction. Marina recognized me, started to smile and wave, then seemed to remember she had to look cool, or hip, or whatever the word was they used now. She sashayed over while I looked around for a reason for her performance. A group of boys watched her cross the street like wolves tracking a lamb. Ah, youth.

"Hi," I said when Marina opened the door and slid in on the passenger side.

"What happened to your car?" Marina asked. She looked pretty disgusted about the old Toyota.

"I told you. It was my ex's."

"Oh, yeah. That's tough." She frowned. "Where have you been? I left a bunch of messages on that stupid machine of yours. Don't you ever go home?"

"Sure. You're supposed to talk after the beep, Marina, not before."

"Yeah?"

"So what's the news?"

"My aunt found a passbook, you know, like for a savings account?"

I nodded.

"She's pissed over it. It's got like forty thousand dollars in it." Marina laughed. "If she could have been this pissed off when he was beating her, I swear, she coulda killed him herself." She laughed again.

"So she didn't know about it?"

"Not hardly. Auntie scrimped every dime she could and all he ever did was gripe. Told her she spent too much. And now she finds this. It's too funny to laugh about."

"Didn't she know about Noni?"

"Not really. I mean she did, and she didn't. If it really came down to it, she'd admit there was somebody, but otherwise, forget it. She just didn't want to know. I tried to tell her and she just acted like she didn't know what I was talking about." She shrugged. "That's just how she is. She won't change."

"Marina, there's something I want to talk to you about."

"Uh-oh. Sounds like a lecture." She reached for the door handle. "Time for me to check out."

I put a hand on her sleeve. "Listen up a minute, will you? Haven't I been straight with you?"

She nodded but kept her eyes on the intersection ahead. When I didn't go on, she turned. "So what do you want me to do?"

"Talk to a friend of mine. Tell him what you've told me."

"This friend, he's a cop, right?"

I nodded.

"No deal. I don't talk to cops."

"Marina, they think I'm sitting on you. And you're sitting on some very big stuff." I handed her the packet of Murieta's blue pages. "You need to give them this and you need to talk to them."

"Forget it. No way." She threw open the car door and ran down the street, ignoring the surprised calls of her girlfriends and the jeering shouts of the boys.

After she disappeared, they all turned to stare at me with undisguised malevolence. I leaned across and pulled the door closed, then locked it. So much for smooth talk.

The group of boys started drifting toward me. The message was clear. No point in hanging around. Marina wasn't likely to come back and apologize. At least not yet. She needed to cool out first.

I started the engine and pulled away, leaving the boys suddenly closer to the girls than they wanted to be.

47

Upstairs in my apartment I sat down, cleared the table, and put the phone in front of me. I could either forget the whole thing and go to my Japanese class or I could call. I pulled out the slip of paper with the number on it and dialed. A voice answered on the third ring.

I took a deep breath. "I'd like to talk to Judge Coyle."

"She's not available. Would you like to leave a message?"

"Is she in court?"

"No, I'm afraid not. Would you like to leave a message?"

"I'll hold. Tell her I'm an acquaintance of Mr. Murieta's."

"One moment, pl—" The secretary clipped herself short when she put me on hold. Music from some symphony floated over the line while I waited and told myself there was no other way.

"Martha Coyle here." The judge's voice was crisp and cautious. "Who is this?"

"I'm an acquaintance of Jake Murieta." There was a

long pause on the other end. "I know what he was doing."

"I'm afraid I don't know what you're talking about."

"I think you do. If you want to discuss an arrangement, meet me at Alta Plaza tonight, behind the tennis courts. Nine o'clock."

"But I—"

"Just be there." I hung up.

It was easy confirmation. Too easy. I closed my eyes and pictured Murieta's bloated, picked-over carcass and took comfort in the fact I'd picked a landlocked place for the meeting. At least I wouldn't end up like that. I laid my head down on the table across my folded arms. I stayed like that for five minutes or more, then I called Philly Post and told him what I planned to do. We talked and shouted at each other for about half an hour, then I went downstairs.

Blackie was waiting for me at his favorite place at the far end of the bar. The stool next to his was empty, so I climbed up on it, flagged the bartender for a beer, and told Blackie what I'd done.

"She bit, didn't she?"

I nodded. The bartender set an Anchor Steam and a glass in front of me, then left. I sat there and stared into space.

"Your heart's not in it, doll."

"I was hoping she wouldn't," I said.

"Yeah. I know what you mean. I hate to see her go down too."

"Maybe I'm wrong."

Blackie snorted. "And maybe you still believe in the Tooth Fairy." He lit a cigarette and blew smoke out through both nostrils. "Why the meet? You've got enough to cook her. The savings account, the list, the maid and the kid to connect 'em up. You even got your motive."

I dipped my finger into a damp spot on the bar and drew circles on the dry, glossy surface. "I guess I'm rebounding from the August deal. It might be overkill, but I want this so tight nobody'll throw it out."

"You think anybody would as it stands?"

I shrugged. "Like you've always said, Blackie, the law's a fickle thing."

"I said it was fucked, not fickle."

I smiled. "Same thing."

Blackie finished his smoke, and after he'd stubbed it out, I said, "It's not fair. I don't understand. She's a judge, for God's sake."

Blackie didn't say anything and I suddenly remembered my beer. I poured it out slowly, tilting the bottle and glass so that the liquid wouldn't foam. I drank half of it down, then looked up.

"You know, Post wants me to wear a wire."

"What'd you tell him?"

"I told him we'll see."

Blackie raised an eyebrow.

"He finally told me the rest about Murieta's autopsy report," I explained. "You know how August said he was killed first, then thrown in the water? Well, somebody karate-chopped him in the throat and collapsed his windpipe. Post said the move doesn't require any kind of strength or force, but it does require precision and speed. It's called the Iron Hand."

"So how's a wire gonna save you?"

I shrugged. "Reinforcements?"

"Reinforcements, shit. One slice and you're dead."

"I take it you don't approve?"

"Damn right. Fuck the cops. I'll back you up."

I shook my head. "No. I need them, Blackie. It's already set up."

48

At the station, I headed straight for Philly Post's office and thought about Blackie's parting words: "When you bring in the cops, you cut off your options." Maybe. But you also gain their technology and all the backup you need.

After leaving Blackie in the bar I'd gone upstairs and checked a couple of catalogs I had lying around the apartment. A simple wire, the no-frills, no-bells-and-whistles variety, was way out of my price range. And if I bought one, I'd need to wait for Blackie to be free so that he could be at the other end. If I'd ever need to use one again, the thing'd probably be obsolete.

No, sometimes working with the cops was working smart. This was one of those times.

I stepped into the Homicide section and caught sight of Philly Post across the room, slouched over his desk. He didn't look happy—but then he never did. I crossed to the glass door, tapped on it, then let myself in. He looked up and scowled.

"What are you doing here?"

"You said I should come early to get wired."

He stood up, took my elbow, and started me back the way I came without saying a word.

"Hey! What's going on? What're you doing?"

"Just come with me," he said out of the side of his mouth.

We reached the hall and he dragged me toward a door midway down, on the right. When we reached it, he pushed me through it and followed me into the stairwell.

"What's going on?"

"I ran it by the Captain," he said.

"Damn! Why? You weren't supposed to—"

"I need to, to use a wire."

"Great!" I let the sarcasm drip off the word.

"He didn't go for it."

I fell back against the cinder block wall and stuck my hands in my pockets. "Now what?"

He shrugged.

"How much did you tell him? Did you tell him it was Martha Coyle?"

"I had to."

"And me?"

He nodded, showing his big white teeth in an open-mouthed scowl. "He said let you screw up on your own. He's still hot over August." He paused. "Come to think of it, I should be too."

"All right, fine." I pushed myself off the wall. "Thanks, anyway." I started for the door, but he blocked it with his big arm.

"Reschedule it. I'm off-duty tomorrow night."

"Would you call her back if it was your gig?"

"If it meant the difference between backup or not, I would."

"And I'm your sister." I pushed his arm away and pulled open the door. "Look," I said. "I've got to go."

"Don't be stupid, Ventana."

"Then, dammit, don't ask me to change the meet."

He stepped out into the hall after me. "Wait."

I kept on walking. "I'll let you know how it turns out," I said over my shoulder.

49

The damp air dropped a fine mist over me that even my insulated anorak couldn't keep out. I'd come a half hour early just to, well, just because it made me feel better—more in control.

There was a bench spotlighted behind the tennis courts, and my eyes were trained on it. That's where I'd like to talk to Coyle. But first I had to make sure she came alone. And from my vantage point at the very top of the soft hill that was Alta Plaza Park, I'd be able to see her drive up.

At the base of the long, grassy slope lay the street with a red zone and a crosswalk at the corner. I guessed that's where Martha Coyle would park if she rode her motorcycle. If she drove her car, well, that was another story. She'd only need a car to haul things around in—large, inanimate things, like bodies.

I stood in the gravel at the foot of a tall cypress and shivered while I watched the cars straggle by, commuters on their way home from working late or from happy hour at some downtown bar.

While I waited, I wondered if maybe I should have listened to Post and rescheduled. Maybe I should have waited until I got hold of Blackie. *It'll be all right,* I told myself, but my stomach tightened up in a zillion little knots.

When my ears picked up a low, rumbling hum, I knew it was Martha Coyle's motorcycle. Adrenaline surged through me. My arms and legs went light, and my stomach tightened down another notch. I trained my eyes on the single-beam headlight gliding down the street toward me. The cycle slowed at the intersection, then accelerated and kept on going. I didn't know whether to be glad or disappointed.

Something on the street caught a passing car's headlight and winked at me. I went stiff and weak all at once. And all over again I started thinking second thoughts. *Not now,* I whispered, then edged forward to get a better look. Two steps. Three. The object behind the station wagon came into full view: one hefty Kawasaki, in all its polished chrome glory.

"Shit." I backed up under the cypress with a horrible sinking feeling. *Martha Coyle was already here.* I scanned the tennis courts, then the clumps of trees and tall shrubs that dotted the rest of the park.

A church bell chimed down the street. I tried to keep my jaws from clenching up and counted the strokes. Nine o'clock. She'd have to show her face soon.

I scoured the slope below. A quarter of the way up the hill, the stairs turned into a simple path with a low border hedge. Too low to hide anybody, but there were plenty of other dark and creepy places where she could be.

Knowing she was out there keyed me up like a rocket. I knew it was just a matter of time, but time was what was killing my nerves. I reached down and clicked on the tape recorder inside my coat pocket in case I wouldn't get a chance to turn it on later. There was no telling what Coyle had planned.

I listened and waited some more, breathing the cool scent of eucalyptus and pine and telling myself I could handle whatever she dished out. Down on the street a car honked, and, muffled by the distance, a fog horn warned the boats out on the Bay. A radio blared from a passing car, then faded.

I didn't hear the movement behind me at first. I didn't see anything, either, but I *sensed* somebody was there. Then I heard the leaves rustle. I spun around, pebbles churning under my shoes. The limbs of a big fuchsia on my right, just below the back side of the hill, shifted and swayed. The wind picked up. I stared hard into the blackness. Nothing.

Something snapped in the shadows to my right, behind a boxy shrub. This time I ducked away from the tree, around the bushes, and made a wide circle down the slope. I came up behind the hulking stand of shrubs and peeked over the top.

Nothing. Nobody.

If she'd been there, she was gone now. I stopped to listen, but I'd jazzed myself up so much, all I could hear was the drumbeat of my own heart.

I climbed back under the cypress again and waited, listening, watching, barely breathing. It wasn't long before I heard movement once more, this time from down below in front of me. I strained to see where she was, but it was too dark. I'd have to get closer.

Creeping downward over the soft grass, I hugged the bushes, held my breath, and prayed I'd see her before she saw me. I was hurrying, trying to get down there before she vanished again. But I should have been paying attention to where I was going. With my eyes fixed on a spot down the slope, I smashed my left knee into something that yielded under my weight. I stumbled, tripped, and landed right on top of it. It felt just like a sandbag—until it moved.

"Ugh!" I jumped to my feet, but the figure sprang up after me, one arm cocked, fist raised.

That was the last thing I saw.

50

The first clue I had that I was still alive was the pungent scent of eucalyptus and pine. Then I realized I was cold. Other sensations followed: my neck ached, my head throbbed, but most of all, my jaw burned like hot lead. I knew I should be happy about feeling the pain, but I couldn't remember why. I opened my eyes. Blackie was crouching over me in the dark.

"Jeezus fucking Christ," he said. Then I remembered.

"What the—eeow! My jaw. Ooooh." I raised myself up on one elbow, pressed my palm to my left cheek, and tried again. "What the hell are you doing here?" If I clenched my teeth when I talked, it didn't hurt as much.

"What the fuck does it look like?" Blackie rose and offered me his hand. "A guy could get killed keeping an eye out for you."

I ignored his hand and pushed myself up off the ground. Standing upright felt odd, like somebody had shifted the world's axis a couple of degrees and forgot to tell me about it.

"Shit." I slumped over to the park bench and shoved

my hands into my pockets. My knuckles hit something hard. The tape recorder. I pulled it out and clicked it off. "How long was I out?"

"A second. Maybe two."

It felt like a week. I stared into the darkness. "Did you see anything?"

"Nah."

I glanced down the hill to the street. "Her motorcycle's still there."

Blackie followed my gaze. "That ain't hers. I saw the fuck who parked it there, doll. It wasn't the judge."

I flexed my neck to one side then the other. It wasn't broken, but it felt like it should have been.

"She stood you up, doll. I been here since eight."

"Shit." I worked my neck some more. "I was sure she'd bite."

Blackie fumbled for a smoke, lit it, and filled the crisp night air with the sweet aroma of burning tobacco. "Tough break."

"Next time I'm keeping the cops out of it."

"Fucking-A right, Ventana. They're shit, and now you know it."

I rubbed my bruised jaw and gave him a significant look. "Maybe I ought to keep you out of it too."

"Hell, I pulled that punch."

"Yeah?" Maybe I was lucky to be alive, but I didn't feel lucky.

"So how'd they fuck up?"

I told him what Post had done.

"Fucking assholes." Blackie dropped his cigarette and crushed it into the gravel under his foot. "Somebody tipped her."

* * *

But Post denied it immediately. He swore up and down only three people in the department knew: him, his boss, and Kendall. I knew Post wouldn't have given it away, and Kendall was too obsequious even to contemplate breaking a rule. That left Post's boss. He was the only one I had reservations about. But in good conscience, I couldn't pin the blame on him either. It was the easy answer. Too obvious.

No, Martha Coyle had reasons of her own for the no-show. Maybe she didn't give a damn if I pulled the plug on her. Maybe she was ready for the gig to be up. Or maybe—and this was the possibility that worried me—maybe she knew something I didn't—something crucial I'd overlooked that would get her off the hook.

51

I popped a cap off an Anchor Steam and looked out my apartment window. It was time to figure out what to do next, but two days of thinking hadn't got me anywhere. My heart wasn't in it. Instead of coming up with plan B or C, all I wanted to do was drink beer and try to figure out what went wrong with plan A.

The Chinese lady across the street was lining up some kind of roots on her windowsill. They were gnarly and looked dried, like mushrooms, only bigger. She emptied a whole can of them while I finished my third beer. When she started dusting them with some kind of orange powder, my phone rang. I considered letting the answering machine take the call, but I picked it up anyway.

"Yeah?"

"Tuxedo Messages?" The voice was high-pitched, feminine. "Did I get the wrong number?"

I cursed Myra for ever leaving town, then tried to inject into my voice a congeniality I didn't really feel. "That's right. Any message, anytime."

"I need one on very short notice," the voice said. "Two thirty this afternoon. Is that possible?"

I glanced at my watch. Ten till two. One minute to scribble the message onto one of Myra's fancy cards, four minutes to wash my face and change into the tux, and five to finish another beer. That would leave me half an hour to get there.

"Where?"

"Fifty-eight Macondray Lane. At Taylor."

I knew where it was. A two-block row of houses buried atop Russian Hill. Exclusive. Private. Accessible only by foot. Taylor would be at the east end. I could drive there in three minutes or walk it in ten.

"No problem. What's the message?" I picked up a pencil from the table and found a blank pad to write on.

"To err is human. Dot. Dot. Dot."

I wrote it down. "That's it?"

"She'll understand."

"Great," I said without enthusiasm. I'd had enough coy little messages to last me a lifetime. I took down the rest of the information I needed, got her name and credit card number, then hung up.

By the time I'd dressed, dabbed some makeup over my bruised jaw, and finished my beer, I'd decided the walk up the hill would do me good. I'd just straightened my bow tie in front of the mirror when somebody knocked at the door.

"Who is it?"

Nobody answered.

"Who's there?"

"Open the fucking door, Ventana."

I flung it open and Blackie sauntered in, cigarette in hand. "I got a couple of ideas, Ventana."

"Yeah?"

He'd been feeling bad and trying to make it up to me ever since he slugged me. Over the last three days he'd bought me two beers and had even asked me for some burglar-alarm advice.

"You want to nail the judge for good?"

"I don't know. Depends. I'm thinking I'll just let the cops take care of it."

He stopped short and dropped a two-inch ash off the end of his cigarette onto the floor. "What the fuck's wrong with you, doll? You know the cops aren't doing shit. They're going to bury this thing. Don't you want to nail her?"

"I'm not really—" He glared at me. "All right, all right. Yes, I do." I checked my watch. "But I've got to do one of Myra's messages up on Macondray right now. We can talk about it when I get back."

He snorted in disgust. "Fuck that shit. This is more important."

"Twenty minutes, Blackie. That's all. Here, have a beer."

He grumbled, but I left him watching the Chinese lady and her mysterious orange powder and headed out the door.

52

Cool, foggy air whipped my cheeks as I started up Union Street, past Washington Square and Mason, then up the hill to Taylor, where I turned left and up again for another half block. There the stairs to Macondray Lane shot straight up two stories from the sidewalk into a forest of overgrown shrubs.

As I went up the wooden steps, I wondered what Blackie's plan was all about. It had to be something tight, something that would nail Martha Coyle to the wall. Something I hadn't already thought of and discarded.

At the top of the stairs a dense thicket lined the uneven cobblestone path. I passed some mailboxes on my left with their corresponding houses stashed out of sight behind the greenery, and counted house numbers. Eight. Twelve. Fourteen. The last one before the stone walk yielded to bricks was number twenty-two.

Up ahead, in a shady canyon of hillside and trees, were more houses and a monster eucalyptus. I noticed a dirt path leading through a gap in the bushes to my right and followed it, more out of curiosity than anything. Five paces put me at the edge of a cliff, where an arm-sized branch formed a natural guardrail just above my waist. The view wasn't grand: a patch of bay, the twin spires of Saints Peter and Paul, Telegraph Hill, and, four stories straight down, the tops of buildings fronting Union Street.

Except for the grinding racket of some construction going on up the block, the place would have been serene. I tried to block out the noise, then remembered the message. If I didn't hurry, I'd be late.

As I started to turn, my foot slipped. I stumbled, grabbed the guardrail branch, and held on. Loose pebbles rattled down the steep slope, then clattered onto a rooftop farther down than I even wanted to contemplate. Maybe chugging that fourth beer hadn't been such a good idea. I pulled myself up to solid footing and was about to breathe a sigh of relief. Then I saw her.

Martha Coyle stood at the edge of the brick path wearing slacks and a navy-blue parka. Her arms hung loose at her sides, but her fingers twitched.

Right away I knew I wasn't in the best place I could be: a secluded area, loud construction, and a three-inch-wide branch between me and a four-story drop. Martha Coyle wasn't going to do anything exotic this time around—she wouldn't have to. No karate chop to the throat for me. Nothing so fast and clean. One shove and I'd have the longest fifteen seconds of my life to imagine what my body was going to look like at the bottom of the hill.

I weighed my options for about one-tenth of a second, then dove under a bush on my right. The judge charged after me, pulled up short to grab the limb I'd been holding on to, and kicked me in the shin. It hurt, but not as much as a four-story fall.

"Come out of there," she hissed, and kicked me again. I glimpsed her eyes over my shoulder. They were a mad-woman's eyes, gleaming with passionate irrationality. I dug myself in deeper, but she dropped to her knees and came after me. Twigs snapped and leaves rustled behind me as we played G.I. Joe through the bushes. I was get-ting more sober by the millisecond.

I pushed through, ignoring the branches tearing at my face and ripping Myra's tuxedo. Something sharp jabbed my knee. A rock. I picked it up and threw it at her, then scrambled on. All I wanted was to put Martha Coyle between me and that cliff. She wouldn't let me, though.

She caught up with me and clamped a hand on my foot. Then she backed up and hauled me with her like she was reeling in a bass. She didn't look that strong—but she was. I held on to everything I could and even cracked her a couple of good ones in the ribs with my heel, but she refused to let go—or stop.

"Wait!" I screamed when we reached the edge of the clearing. "Wait, dammit!" We were about three feet from the cliff. "I can help you!"

Martha Coyle hesitated, puffing, breathless. I know she didn't mean to, but her grip on my ankle relaxed. That was my ticket. I jerked my foot away and sprang out at her. I shoved her backward against the limb, intending to use Blackie's right hook, but she slid out of my hands and over the edge. I dropped to my knees and pinned her flailing arms to the ground before they could vanish over the cliff.

"Uurgh!" she grunted. "H-h-help! Help me!" She clawed at the dirt while I kicked my legs out behind me and held on to her wrists. She was heavy—solid muscle.

"Hold on!" I shouted. "Be still." But she kept wran-gling and squirming, and her weight pulled me forward in spite of myself. My hands, clutching her arms, disappeared over the ledge. *"Be still, dammit."*

Her fingers found the sleeves of my jacket and worked up my arm, an inch at a time, while her legs fought for a foothold. Her body seemed to buck against the sheer wall of rock.

"Hold on," I whispered, then dug my toes in behind me. Slowly I inched my way back. I knew I could save her; I'd seen it done a million times before in old reruns of *Combat.*

With my arms straight out in front of me, I pulled Coyle with me. Her wrists came over the edge first, then her forearms. Then her head and shoulders. Her elbows dug into the ground, and her grip on my arms loosened.

"Don't let go!" I shouted. She grunted and held on. "Come on. *Come on.*"

"Ugh!" She hauled her torso over the edge, then swung a leg over. I sat up, grabbed her knee and elbow, and dragged her with me, backward toward the brick path, away from certain death. She clung to my arms until I finally pried her fingers out of my flesh. If it weren't for my jacket, she probably would have pulled the skin right off my arms.

I dropped her in a crumpled heap by the walk, her body heaving, head down, sucking air and making little grunting noises while I bent over her, arms on my knees, trying to catch my own breath. At least I'd gotten what I wanted: she was between me and the cliff.

I noticed her parka again, then I realized why it had caught my attention: it was the same jacket the City College mugger wore.

"Are you all right?" I asked.

Her quivering shoulders straightened, and our eyes met.

"You should have stayed out of it," she said between breaths. Her voice was flat and hard. I hadn't expected gratitude, but I thought we'd at least reached a truce.

"You need help," I said.

She laughed bitterly and shook her head.

"Look, I know what happened to you in law school. I know why you hired Jake Murieta."

Martha Coyle's face was still flushed from the exertion, but her eyes were cold and dead. She didn't say a word.

I took a deep breath. My heartbeat was almost back to normal. "You hired him to kill men you thought deserved to die, men who were convicted and sent to prison but got out on early parole, men who fit the description of those who—who raped you." I stared down into Martha Coyle's face. Behind that hard, evil edge, inside, somewhere, she had to be hurting. She *had* to be. I realized I was shivering.

"How did you find out?" she asked stiffly.

"I've seen those blue envelopes you gave him. And his—"

"No, no. How did you find out about *me*? About . . . law school?"

"It wasn't hard to put it together once I knew what Jake Murieta was doing." For some reason I wanted to spare her knowing that I'd read her medical file. "Look, you need help. Why—"

"They left me for dead," she snarled. Her whole frame shook. "Do you know what it's like? *Do you?*"

I didn't answer. I didn't have an answer.

"Law school saved me," she said. "It gave me a purpose. I became a prosecutor and I won every rape case I argued. But the sentences the judges handed down weren't ever enough. I knew justice would never be served unless I could pass the sentences myself."

Her eyes sparkled weirdly, and the wind kicked up. Either the cold or the raw hatred in Martha Coyle's face made me shiver again.

"You don't know what it was like," she said. "Those men . . . what they did . . . what they did to all the women who came to court for justice. I tried. It didn't matter how long a sentence I gave them, they'd be out too soon. The system doesn't work."

"Your system doesn't work, either, Judge Coyle. I understand why you did what you did, but that doesn't make it right. You've got to turn yourself—"

Without warning she lunged at me. Her right arm flew up, then drew back in a perfect arch. The flat blade of her hand flashed white. Just as her hand shot toward my throat, I blocked her thrust with my own forearm.

When bone met bone, something snapped. I didn't feel anything at first, then a sharp, numbing pain spread up my arm from wrist to shoulder.

It took me a split second to register that my arm was probably broken. Then I reached out and locked both arms around the judge in a bear hug. My broken arm throbbed, but I grabbed it above the break and squeezed as hard as I could without passing out.

"You fool," she hissed in my ear. She was squirming, breathing hot on my face. "I did it for *you,* for all the women, to free them to the night. You should be grateful. Umph!" She worked an arm between us and pushed against me. I held on.

"Let go of me!" she screamed. Then she spat in my face and kicked me in the shin.

It was the kick that did it. Her toe found the same spot she'd nailed in the bushes. I let go and hauled back to punch her with my good arm, but she was ready for me. She was fast, faster than anything I'd ever seen. She did a little hop and took a spinning step that sent her foot through the air. It connected on the right side of my jaw with a crack that rattled my teeth and my brains. Blackie *had* pulled his punch.

I backed up, staggering and breathless. The world was suddenly out of focus. My life didn't exactly play through my head, but I felt like it should have. I wanted to see all the good times one more time before that chop hit my throat. It was coming; I knew it was just a matter of time.

A rustling whirl in front of me made me lift my head and blink to focus. Martha Coyle was moving in for the kill. Her arms were weaving deadly patterns through the air as she closed in on me. She was only two feet away now, and her arm was drawn back.

I lunged forward, rammed my heel into her instep and landed a tight left hook under her jaw with my good arm.

The force of the blow sent her backward, but she recovered faster than I thought she would and came at me again, angrier than a crazy tiger. This time I was ready, though. I tucked my chin down and dodged to one side when she jumped at me, her feet and hands whirling at me like circles of death.

As she flew past me, her muscular little body glanced off my shoulder and jarred my broken arm. It hurt like hell, but I managed to reach out with my one good arm to give the judge's back a rock-solid shove. The unexpected momentum threw her off balance. She landed and stumbled, and when she tried to right herself, she fell forward. Her head banged against the monster eucalyptus, and she dropped with an "Ummph!" into a still, harmless heap.

"Not bad," a raspy voice said from behind me. I jerked my head around in time to see Blackie crawl out from behind a blooming bush not more than ten feet away.

"Blackie! Thank God!"

He grinned at me. "Great left hook, doll. You all in one piece?"

"Sort of. Why didn't you help me out?"

He gave me a disapproving look. "Two against one?" he said. "Nah, you were doing all right."

I started to laugh, then winced when I tried to move my arm. I staggered over to the tree and stared down at the crumpled figure at my feet. Blackie came up behind me. I heard him light a cigarette, then smelled the smoke as he exhaled with a loud sigh.

"Too bad about her," he said. "The lady had class."

I thought of the strong, self-assured woman I'd met just the week before. I remembered the costumed dominatrix in Pete August's bedroom, then tried to imagine the horrified victim she must have been years ago when four savage young men destroyed her life.

"Yeah," I said. "Too bad."

53

Sitting across from Philly Post's desk, the plaster of my arm cast barely dry, I gave the lieutenant a reproachful look.

"Aren't you at least going to thank me?"

"For screwing up my career?"

"To hear you tell it, Post, I can't breathe without messing things up for you. I caught the killer, didn't I? You had your chance to be in on it."

"The Captain looks like a real asshole."

"That's his fault. You don't look so bad."

"Yeah, right. Tell him that while he's clawing his way out of the toilet you put him in."

I started to laugh, but groaned instead when the pain shot up through my jaw. He looked up. "You're lucky it's not broken."

"Come on, Philly, where's your sense of humor? Did you talk to Maximum Marks?"

"Didn't have to. Pete explained when he came down. Judge Marks is saving that shit for when his wife gets better. He thinks she'll be able to make the guys some-day."

"Poor man."

Post looked out over my shoulder past the glass door and frowned. "Shit."

I turned and spotted Blackie stalking through the maze of cluttered desks toward Philly's office.

"What's Coogan doing here? Kendall took his state-ment down at Macondray."

"I asked him to pick me up. You guys dragged me into that ambulance, then hauled me down here. How was I supposed to get home?"

"I would have—"

Blackie walked in without knocking. He ignored Post and grinned at me. Philly Post cleared his throat. "We're wrapping up a statement here," he said.

Blackie glared back at him. "So?"

"So sit down and shut up till we're done."

Blackie puffed up his chest and sputtered, ready to square off—or at least yell at him—but I surprised him when I laughed out loud.

"Oh, sit down, Blackie," I said. "We're all grown-ups here."

He didn't look happy, but he sat down anyway. Philly started to say something, but Blackie interrupted.

"She sure was a scrapper," he told me. "Did she talk when she came to?" It was like Post wasn't even there.

I glanced over at Post and winked, so he gave up and leaned back in his chair to rub his eyes.

"Under the expert inquiries of Lieutenant Post, here," I said. Blackie snorted, but I managed to get a semblance of a smile from Post. "And with Marina Murieta's state-ment, Judge Coyle admitted to hiring Murieta. When she realized in the hospital that the gig was up, she confessed to Murieta and Wilson and the rest."

"I don't get it. Why pop the guy who was doing her dirty work? Was he giving her static?"

"He had had one too many and had let Wilson in on it," I explained. "Wilson saw money in a blackmail scheme, so he tried it out on her. All that bought him was a swim in China Basin, and Murieta's in the Bay."

"What about August?"

"She told him they were blackmailing her over their idea of fun-and-games in bed. He didn't have a clue as to what was really going on."

"What a babe," Blackie said.

"When she ran into you downstairs and you told her I saw August kill Murieta, she went ahead and fixed it to look like he really did kill him."

"My ex-wife was like that," Blackie said, and shook his head. "I didn't have a clue about her either. What about Purdue?"

I flashed a rueful look at Post. "It looks like Purdue died of natural causes after all."

Post cleared his throat again. "Are you about done?" he asked Blackie, then glanced pointedly at his watch. "It's Sunday, you know."

Blackie glared at him and kept on talking. "So how'd she know you were doing the tux gig?"

"She followed me and got the number off a card I left with one of the messagees."

Philly Post stood up behind his desk. "We'll have to finish up tomorrow," he said. I stood too.

"I'll only come back if you do me a favor," I said.
"Sure."

I caught Blackie's eye. "What about you?"

Blackie squinted at me. "What are you getting at?"

"I want you two to shake hands."

"Aw, come on, Ventana," Post protested.

"Lay off it, doll. I'll eat shit first."

"Will you two stop acting like a couple of schoolboys? What's it going to hurt to treat each other like decent people?"

They glared at each other. Neither one of them said a word. Neither one of them made a move.

I waited. "Well?"

Post shifted on his feet, then made a motion forward with his hand. "What do you say?" he said, "We can always wash our hands down the hall when we're done."

Blackie hesitated until I winked at him. Then he reached across the desk and chuckled. "What the hell?"

GLORIA WHITE lives in San Francisco.
Murder on the Run is her first novel.